SECRETS
FROM THE
Past

Books by
Jenny Elaine

Rose of Savannah Series

The Healing Rose of Savannah
The Whispering Shadows of Savannah

A Shady Pines Mystery Series

Secrets from the Past
Lost in the Past
Storms of the Past

A SHADY PINES MYSTERY – BOOK 1

SECRETS FROM THE *Past*

JENNY ELAINE

ISBN: 979-8-9853661-0-5

PROLOGUE

Cora slowly walked up the stairs leading to the second floor, the steaming mug of fresh, hot coffee she carried warming her icy hands. It was late, and a storm was brewing; she could hear the rumble of thunder off in the distance. Perhaps that's why he was so late; he'd gotten caught in the storm.

With a sigh, Cora pushed open the door to one of the guest bedrooms and stepped inside. The house was empty and still, without the usual sound of chatter and movement from the guests, and she decided to air out some of the rooms while she waited for him to arrive.

Setting her coffee cup on the dresser, she went over to the window and opened it. The sound of the wind whipping through the pine trees sent a sudden chill of foreboding down her spine. Normally, the sound was peaceful and relaxing, but something felt different tonight.

Pulling her sweater tighter around her shoulders, Cora stood at the window for a while, so deep in thought that she failed to notice the soft tread of footsteps coming slowly up the stairs and down the hall. When a shadow stepped into the doorway, she spun around, squinting through the darkness at the large, black silhouette. She hadn't turned on the lights in the bedroom, but the glow from the hallway illuminated his face just enough, and her smile melted away when she saw who it was.

"What…what are you doing here?" She gasped in a hoarse whisper, her fingers gripping the sweater so tightly she could barely feel them any longer.

"You know what I want, Cora," he said as he stepped forward, the sound of his voice making her skin crawl.

"I told you, 'No'," she hissed, backing away from him, her shoulders bumping against the window frame. "Why can't you just leave me alone?"

The thunder rumbled yet again, the sound much closer this time, and when the lightning flashed, Cora saw his face clearly and the look in his eyes told her that her fate was sealed.

Before she could scream, he lunged forward and wrapped his hand around her throat. She tried to fight, to get away from this monster who was trying to destroy everything good in her life, but it was too late. She'd made a horrible mistake long ago, and now she would pay for it.

CHAPTER 1

W*elcome to Shady Pines, population 2,458*

It was nearly eight o'clock in the evening when Misty Raven drove past the welcome sign and entered the small, southeastern Georgia town. The sun had set and there was only the tiniest bit of light left in the sky; as Misty drove down Main Street, she noticed that all the stores were closed for the night. This was how she'd planned her arrival, when everyone was home and not out and about to notice a stranger arriving in town. No one in Shady Pines knew her or her reasons for coming here, but she knew how nosy small-town folks could be and didn't wish to answer any prying questions just yet. She needed some time to settle in first.

Easing her foot off the gas pedal, Misty drove slowly as she carefully took in her surroundings, noting the row of buildings on either side with overhead signs that read: "Shady Pines Pharmacy", "Barlow Hardware Store", "Local Feed and Grain" and "Dilly Dally's Gift Shop". This was her first visit to Shady Pines, and yet it was now her new home…for a little while, at least.

7

It would take some time, just as it always did, but she would discover soon enough if this was the place she'd been searching for.

Misty turned off the main road and drove a couple of miles out of town until she came to a long, dirt road with rows of pine trees on either side. The road was bumpy and full of potholes, and there were no streetlights to be found. The night steadily grew darker under the shade of the tree branches, casting shadows all around. Finally, through the headlights, Misty saw the old place come into view, and she parked by the front porch. She pulled a flashlight from the glove compartment, dug around for the house key, and then climbed from the car, jumping back when she realized she'd stepped into an ant bed. Leaves crunched beneath her feet, and she stood silently for a moment, listening. It was eerily quiet, with only the chirps of a few frogs and crickets to break the stillness of the night.

Maybe arriving at night wasn't such a good idea after all, she thought, fighting off a sudden chill as she reached up to touch the heart-shaped locket around her neck. She'd had the locket for many years, and it was somehow always a source of comfort to her.

With a deep breath, Misty squared her shoulders and walked around her car, pointing the flashlight's beam at the old building as she slowly took in the magnificent Queen Anne Victorian style of architecture that rose up before her like a graceful relic from the past. The house was built in 1886 and sported the typical L-shaped wraparound porch, steep roof with a front-facing gable, and overhanging eaves. According to the real estate agent, this place was once the most beautiful spot in southeastern Georgia, but the obvious disrepair in which it had fallen through the years was astounding. Once a glorious bright white, the house was now a shabby gray, with chipped paint and rotting boards. Shutters drooped, several windows were broken, vines crept along the outer walls like snakes, and the shrubs were so overgrown Misty could hardly see the floor of the porch. The real estate agent said the house had been uninhabited for fifteen years, and the previous owners had done no renovations since the early eighties. Misty hadn't, however, counted on it being quite so rundown.

What have I gotten myself into? She asked herself, shaking her head as she slowly walked up the rickety front porch steps. She placed the key into the rusty old lock, and with a squeak, the door swung open of its own accord. The front hall was dark and full of cobwebs; with a deep breath, Misty stepped inside, the floorboards groaning beneath her feet as she made her way through her new home. Old floral wallpaper that had once been bold and vibrant now hung in faded shreds upon the walls; Misty stopped before a gold-plated mirror, barely able to see her reflection in the cracked, smudged glass.

Oh, the stories this place could tell, she thought as she continued on through the house, taking in what remained of an old sofa with holes in the cushions, a bookshelf with a handful of dusty books scattered along its shelves, and a staircase with broken spindles in the handrail that led to the second floor. If ever there was a model for a haunted house, this would be it.

Suddenly, Misty heard the sound of footsteps and caught her breath. Someone was walking along the porch; she could hear it creaking as the person circled around the house, but the real estate agent said there were no close neighbors living nearby. With the thought that it could be a vagrant and she should have locked the front door behind her, Misty began making her way back to the front of the house to do just that when she heard the now familiar squeak of the front door as it swung open. With her heart in her throat, Misty peered around the corner to find a hunched-over, dark silhouette standing in the doorway.

"What are you doing here?" A raspy voice spoke out, the sound echoing off the bare walls, and Misty took a step back at the tone of displeasure in the man's voice.

"I...I own this place," she stammered, swallowing past the sudden dryness in her throat.

The man stepped inside, and the beam from Misty's flashlight illuminated his face, revealing wrinkled skin, a pinched expression, and brown eyes narrowed in suspicion. He was quite elderly, with wispy white hair that hung over his collar, and suspenders held his drooping pants in place.

"What do you mean?" He asked with a frown. "I didn't know anyone had bought this place. Who are you?"

"My name is Misty Raven, and I purchased this house last week," Misty stated, relieved to find that if this man intended to cause trouble, he was too old to put up much of a fight. Raising an eyebrow, she cleared her throat and asked, "Who are *you*?"

He stared at her for a moment without answering, and Misty began to fidget uncomfortably. Finally, he said, "I'm Loren Thomas. I live in the woods behind this place. Why have you come here? I can't imagine why anyone would want to buy this old dump."

Deciding that her new neighbor wasn't a threat but merely a nosy, disgruntled old man, Misty said politely, "I renovate old houses, Mr. Thomas. When I saw this home listed online, I didn't want to miss such a wonderful opportunity." Glancing around the room, she added with a sigh, "I didn't, however, realize just how much work it was going to need. The real estate agent led me to believe it wasn't in very bad shape."

"Young people," Mr. Thomas huffed, shaking his head. "Didn't you ever think you should have come out to see the place first before you bought it?"

No, because this is the only place for sale

around here and therefore my only option.

She stopped herself before uttering those words, and instead forced a smile and said, "I like to think of it as a challenge, Mr. Thomas. Before long, this place will be as beautiful as ever."

Raising an eyebrow, Mr. Thomas took a step closer and said in a low, almost sinister tone, "You do know that this place is haunted, don't you? That's why no one else ever bought it."

Blinking, Misty took a step back and stammered, "W-what? Oh…no, I didn't know that…but I don't believe in such things."

With a shrug, Mr. Thomas turned and walked from the room, throwing over his shoulder, "Don't say I didn't warn you."

Misty stood in the middle of the large, open room and watched as her neighbor walked through the house and out the way he'd come, slamming the door behind him. He apparently didn't want her here, and she wondered why. Would everyone in this town be so uninviting? If so, it may take longer than she'd hoped to find what she was looking for.

Misty waited a bit before going back out into the dark night to retrieve her purse and suitcase, and when she did, she couldn't seem to force Mr. Thomas's words from her mind.

You do know that this place is haunted, don't you?

Just as she'd told him before, Misty didn't believe in such things, but as she settled in for the night, she found herself feeling uneasy and decided to get the electricity turned on as soon as possible.

As soon as she drifted off to sleep, one of her dreams started forming in her muddled brain. She hadn't had one in months, but it was the same as it always was. The images were dark and blurry, while flashes of light bounced overhead, almost like that of street lights. She was being carried in someone's arms and could hear the sound of heavy breathing as they seemed to be running from something…or someone. Footsteps echoed along what sounded like gravel or cement, and just up ahead, something rose up through the darkness, but Misty couldn't quite make out what it was.

During these dreams, Misty always felt tense and afraid; she just didn't know why. When she woke up the next morning, she wondered what it was about this place that seemed to have stirred up the secret that lay in the deep recesses of her mind.

CHAPTER 2

The electrician came over the next afternoon, and while he worked, Misty opened all the windows to air the place out and started cleaning. She knew that once she began with the renovations, the house would become filthy all over again, but she refused to work in a place filled with cobwebs and dust so thick she could see her own footprints on the floor.

"You're going to have to replace most of the wiring," Adam Dawson, the electrician, told her later when he found her scrubbing the kitchen counter. "It's pretty old and hasn't been used in fifteen years, so I'm afraid it could be dangerous."

"I figured," Misty said with a sigh. "How long do you think that would take?"

"I can have it done in a week," Adam said as he wiped his dusty hands on an old rag he pulled from his pocket. Well-built and very tall, he had short, dark hair and a strong jawline.

"When can you get started?" Misty wanted to know.

Adam pulled his cellphone from his shirt pocket and checked his schedule. "Would tomorrow be soon enough?" He asked with a smile, his black eyes sparkling.

"Tomorrow would be perfect," Misty replied

with a sigh of relief.

As she walked him out, Adam asked, "You're going to do all the renovations yourself?"

"Most of them," Misty replied. "I'm pretty handy with tools."

"You must be," he said, looking at her admiringly. "If you need any help, I would be happy to make some recommendations."

"I would appreciate that. Thank you."

With a smile, Misty waved goodbye to Adam and closed the door, pleased to know that not everyone in this town was as unfriendly as her neighbor, Mr. Thomas.

While Adam and his crew worked, Misty spent the next four days cleaning the house from top to bottom. There was hardly any furniture, and what remained was too old and broken down to use. She'd been sleeping on a mattress on the floor, and by the end of the fourth day, the house was clean enough to start renovating.

With a long list of needed supplies, Misty drove into town the next morning to visit the hardware store. When she walked inside, the bell above the door jingled loudly, and the handful of people milling about turned to glance her way. She retrieved a buggy and pushed it towards the nail aisle, not missing the curious looks and whispers from those she passed.

Eager to get away from the stares, Misty quickened her steps and had just rounded the corner of the aisle when her buggy connected with the solid metal leg of a ladder. Before she could even blink, the ladder toppled, and a blur of blue plaid, flailing arms, and white boxes filled with nails flashed before her eyes just as it all came spilling to the ground with a loud, resounding *crash*.

"What on earth…"

The mumbled groan snapped Misty from the shocked daze she was in, and she hurriedly stepped over the ladder to kneel beside the man that was lying on the floor, holding his head and moaning.

"I'm so sorry," she said, reaching out with trembling fingers to touch his arm. "I didn't know anyone was there…"

"You would have seen me if you hadn't come racing around the corner like a thoroughbred in the Kentucky Derby," the man mumbled in irritation.

People had gathered around to see what the commotion was about, and Misty felt her cheeks flush with embarrassment.

"I *said* I was sorry," she stated, standing to her feet as the man pushed himself upward.

"Brice, are you okay?" A man in his mid-sixties called out as he pushed his way through the crowd.

With pursed lips, "Brice" looked at the mess on the floor and said with a sigh, "Just peachy."

"Mr. Barlow, this young lady here went gallivanting around the corner and knocked poor

Brice right off of his ladder," a middle-aged woman spoke out, eyeing Misty with a sniff.

Clearing his throat, Mr. Barlow said, "Well, I'm sure it was just an accident, and if y'all wouldn't mind giving us some room, we'll get this mess cleaned up."

With raised eyebrows and a lot of murmuring, the shoppers walked away and returned to their business. *I should have just stayed at the house*, Misty thought as she bent down to help gather the nails.

"Don't worry about cleaning this up, ma'am," Mr. Barlow said, touching Misty gently on the shoulder. "Brice and I will get it. Won't we, Brice?"

Brice said nothing as he moved the ladder from the middle of the aisle and placed it in a nearby corner. He'd just returned to kneel at Misty's side when the telephone rang, and Mr. Barlow hurried off to answer it, leaving the two alone.

"You really should let us clean this up," Brice said after a moment, breaking the awkward silence.

Thinking that he was trying to be nice, Misty glanced up to respond but stopped when he continued with, "Who knows what else you'll destroy if you hang around."

Her eyes widening, Misty opened her mouth to give him a piece of her mind when his face broke into a grin and he said with a chuckle, "I'm joking. Don't look so fierce; it's scaring me a little."

Brice winked and got back to work, leaving Misty to stare at the top of his head with just a bit of irritation. "Well, you know how fierce us thoroughbreds can be," she replied drolly.

His lips twitching, Brice cleared his throat and said, "I apologize for saying that; I wasn't thinking clearly, and the words just sort of popped out." Holding out his hand, he said, "Let's start over, shall we? I'm Brice Barlow."

After a brief hesitation, Misty took his hand and said, "I'm Misty Raven."

"You're the one who just bought the old bed-and-breakfast, aren't you?" Brice asked.

"Word travels fast around here," Misty stated, reaching for a box for Brice to place the nails into. Pausing, she looked at him and said in a surprised tone, "I didn't realize it used to be a bed-and-breakfast."

Brice nodded, a lock of sandy-colored hair falling across his forehead. "Yes, ma'am, about fifteen years ago before it closed."

Her brow furrowing, Misty tilted her head and asked, "Why hasn't anyone bought it since then? It has the potential to be a really beautiful place."

Brice stopped to look at her, his dark blue eyes serious as he asked, "No one told you?"

Misty shook her head, and with a sigh, Brice said, "Well then, just forget I said anything."

"You're not going to tell me it's haunted, too, are you?" She asked, cocking an eyebrow in his direction.

"Not exactly," Brice replied with a chuckle.

They'd successfully gathered all the nails and placed them back into the boxes, and Brice took Misty's elbow as they both stood up.

"Look," he said, going back to retrieve the ladder, "why don't I help you find everything you need, and we can go get some coffee afterward? I'll tell you everything you want to know."

Misty hesitated, pondering the request. She'd always been a loner and wasn't the type to make friends easily, but she'd come to this town for a reason, and in order to find the answers she was seeking, she was going to have to be friendly.

"Okay, it's a deal," she replied with a smile.

An hour later, Brice helped Misty load her vehicle with several gallons of paint, nails, two-by-fours, sandpaper, hardware, light fixtures, and various other necessary items. She would have to hire a plumber soon, but for now, she had everything she needed to get started.

"Ready to get that cup of coffee?" Brice asked as Misty closed the back of her car and locked it.

"Lead the way," she told him, grabbing her purse from the cart.

They strolled along the sidewalk, a cool breeze ruffling Misty's naturally curly black hair around her shoulders. She reached into her purse and retrieved a hair tie, pulling her thick mane into a low ponytail. It was always very warm in southeastern Georgia during the summer months, but fall was just around the corner and the weather was cooling off a bit.

"So, I'm curious about something," Brice said, glancing over at Misty. "Why would anyone move to a town they've never been to and buy a dilapidated old building they've never even seen?"

"How do you know I've never been here?" She asked, raising her eyebrows at him.

"Because I'd remember it if you had," he replied with a sly smile.

Chuckling, Misty said, "Buying old homes to renovate and sell is just what I do."

"Short and to the point," Brice said, pursing his lips. "You don't add much embellishment, do you?"

"Only to the homes I renovate," she replied, her blue-gray eyes twinkling, and Brice laughed.

"Where are you originally from?" He wanted to know.

"You ask a lot of questions," Misty stated.

"Sorry," Brice chuckled, opening the door to the little coffee shop.

"Brice Barlow, you're late," a voice called out from behind the counter, and Misty glanced over to see a striking young woman smiling at her companion.

"Yeah, well, we had a bit of an incident over at the store," he replied, winking at Misty as they approached the counter.

"You must be the one responsible for the death of Pop's old ladder," the woman said, her eyes twinkling as she smiled at Misty. "I've been telling him to get rid of that thing for ages."

"Pop's ladder is fine," Brice stated, leaning a hip against the counter. "I, on the other hand, saw my life flash before my eyes."

"You look just fine to me," the woman stated drolly, eyeing Brice with a cocked brow.

"You've already heard about the accident?" Misty asked the woman, her eyes wide.

"News travels fast in a small town," she said with a laugh. Reaching across the counter, she held out her hand and said, "I'm Tori Barlow, Brice's cousin."

"It's nice to meet you," Misty said, shaking Tori's hand. "I'm…"

"Misty Raven," Tori interrupted with a smile. "I've heard. What brings you to our fair city, Misty? Other than buying the old bed-and-breakfast, of course."

"That's exactly what I've been trying to find out," Brice spoke up, his lips twitching as he eyed Misty.

"As I told Brice, this is what I do for a living, and when I saw the listing for the beautiful old house online, I just couldn't resist." Misty shrugged, smiling innocently.

Tori seemed to sense that Misty didn't wish to answer any more questions and changed the subject. While Misty eyed the selection of delicious looking cakes and pastries under the counter, she listened as the two cousins talked. She liked Tori, and the fact that she ran the local coffee house and probably knew everything about everyone just made forming a friendship with her even more appealing.

After choosing a slice of homemade cheesecake and an iced coffee, Misty joined Brice at a corner table and immediately took a bite of the deliciously creamy dessert.

"So, you promised to tell me about the house," she said after a moment.

"You don't waste any time, do you?" He chuckled. Leaning back in his chair, Brice crossed one leg over the other and began the story. "Back when the place was still open, the owner, a woman named Cora Griffin, started dating a man named Hank Johnson. The two were supposed to be married, but suddenly had a falling out a week before the wedding and Cora called it off. Two days later, she was found lying on the ground just below one of the upstairs windows; the police said it was most likely suicide. When they started looking for Hank, they discovered that he'd disappeared. They searched and searched for months, but never found him."

Eyes wide, Misty asked, "Do you think she killed herself because she was heartbroken over the engagement?"

"I don't know," Brice replied, shrugging his broad shoulders.

"But where did Hank disappear to?" Misty wanted to know, her brow wrinkling. "He hasn't come back after all these years?"

Leaning forward, Brice lowered his voice and said, "Some people wondered if he killed Cora and that's why he disappeared, but I guess we'll never know."

Her imagination igniting, Misty asked, "Was there a suicide note?"

"No."

Misty took a sip of her coffee, pondering the story for a moment. She'd always had an overactive imagination, and when such an interesting subject was broached, she couldn't help but want to uncover the truth. Setting her cup back on the table, she asked, "So, this is why people say the house is haunted? Because Cora Griffin died there?"

"Rumors began spreading around town that it's cursed, and your neighbor, Mr. Thomas, didn't help matters when he started telling people he saw Cora's ghost through the upstairs windows at night," Brice said with a sigh. "The place eventually became so run down no one was even trying to sell it until that new real estate agent took an interest and posted it online."

"What a sad story," Misty said, propping her chin against her fist. "I guess we'll never know what happened to poor Miss Griffin."

"Well, maybe now that you're sprucing the place up, her ghost will be able to rest in peace," Brice stated teasingly.

That night, Misty was deep in thought as she walked slowly through the dark house, the creaks and groans beneath her feet louder than usual. She didn't want to admit it, but Brice's story had left her feeling a bit uneasy. Oh, not the rumors of the house being cursed or Mr. Thomas's nonsense about seeing a ghost, but the fact that someone had quite possibly been murdered in this house. Brice said the police thought it was suicide, but Misty suspected otherwise. If Cora killed herself, wouldn't she have left a suicide note? And if she really was murdered, that meant her killer was still out there.

CHAPTER 3

"Wow, it's amazing how much of a change you've already made in this room. It looks great."

Turning to look at Adam, Misty smiled over her shoulder and said, "Thank you. It's a work in progress. Once I finish in here, I've got the rest of the house waiting for me."

Over the course of the last week, Misty had sanded down the kitchen cabinets and painted them a soft shade of blue. She'd also refinished the hardwood floor, bringing out the beautiful red and brown hues that glistened in the temporary lighting Adam had so graciously set up for her. She was now about to sand down the walls to prepare them for a fresh coat of paint and was in the process of laying out drop cloths all along the floor.

"I can only imagine how beautiful the house is going to look once you're finished," Adam said. Holding out an envelope, he placed it on the counter and added, "Here is your bill. I'm finished, so you should be good to go."

With a squeal of excitement, Misty ran to the doorway and flipped up the light switch, her eyes bright as the overhead bulb blinked to life, illuminating the room in a soft glow.

"This will be so much better than working by

lamp light," she said with a sigh of relief. Turning to smile at Adam, she added, "Thank you so much for all of your hard work."

"It was my pleasure," he replied warmly, reaching out to shake her hand.

As Misty walked him out, she tucked a stray curl behind her ear and asked, "Does the town have a library? I haven't had the chance to do much exploring, so I'm afraid I don't know my way around yet."

"We sure do," Adam nodded, and proceeded to give her directions. "Now that you've got electricity, though, you can get Wi-Fi out here."

"Oh, I want to look through some old newspapers and stuff," Misty blurted out before she could stop herself. When Adam looked at her curiously, she shrugged and said nonchalantly, "If I'm going to live here, I need to get acquainted with the town's past, right?"

"True, but it wouldn't hurt to get acquainted with its present, too," he replied, a flirtatious grin pulling at his lips. Clearing his throat, he asked, "Would you like to go out with me sometime? I'd be more than happy to show you around and share the history of the town with you."

"What a kind offer," Misty said, relieved that Adam didn't press her about the newspaper comment. "I'd like that very much."

"How about this Saturday? I could pick you up at six."

"It's a date," she nodded, instantly berating

herself inwardly for using the word "date". Adam had simply asked to show her around town; he had said nothing about a date, and Misty didn't wish to give him the wrong idea.

"I'll see you then," he said with a satisfied smile, sauntering out to his truck with a tune whistling past his lips.

Way to go, Raven, she thought with a sigh. She'd never been the smooth type when it came to men, which was another reason she always kept to herself. Socially awkward was what most people called it, and Misty thought the term to be quite fitting.

The next morning, Misty went to the library. She wore a baseball cap and glasses, but suspected the librarian still knew who she was. It didn't seem that many strangers passed through Shady Pines very often, and when they did, they certainly didn't stop at the library.

After speaking with the librarian, Misty was directed to a microfilm reader. She was relieved to find that it was located in a private corner at the far end of the library, as she didn't want anyone passing by to see what she was researching.

Touching the locket around her neck, Misty began her search. It was long and tedious work, and by the time she finished, she'd barely made any progress. She'd flipped through page after page of an endless row of newspapers, but still hadn't found what she was looking for. *You'll just have to come back and try again later,* she told herself with a sigh.

As Misty headed home, the sun was going down and the town was turning in for the night. When her stomach suddenly pinched and rumbled loudly, she realized with a sigh that she had eaten nothing since breakfast. She pulled in front of her house and parked. Her mind was so focused on making supper that she didn't realize anything was amiss until she opened the front door and stepped inside.

The house was dark and quiet, with the ever present sound of the wind whispering through the pine trees outside, but Misty immediately sensed that she wasn't alone. Hurriedly, she fumbled for the lights. Before her fingers could find the switch, the sound of breaking glass shattered the silence and Misty jumped back with a gasp, her shoulder bumping painfully against the doorframe. Just then, she heard footsteps hurrying out the back door. With her heart in her throat, she grasped along the wall until she finally found the light switch. Flipping it upward, the overhead lights clicked on, and Misty spun around to hurry into the living room on trembling legs, her eyes widening at the sight before her. There, just across the room on the wall, was a message written in red paint. It said, "LEAVE WHILE YOU STILL CAN".

The police arrived at Misty's house in record

time. Shaken and frazzled, Misty met them out on the front porch, her body trembling all over and mind racing in a thousand directions. Who had been in her house, and why did they want her to leave?

"You're sure you didn't see anyone?" Officer Lewis asked after he'd thoroughly searched the house. A slender-built man in his mid-fifties, he stood at an average height with a fringe of brown hair that rimmed an otherwise bald head.

"It was too dark," Misty replied, rubbing her bare arms. "I couldn't see anyone."

"Looks like whoever it was knocked over this glass jar," the other officer called out, pointing to the empty jar of tea Misty had left sitting on the fireplace that morning.

Suddenly, the floor creaked from behind, and they all spun to find Mr. Thomas lurking in the doorway.

"What are you doing here?" Misty wanted to know, her voice trembling as she eyed her neighbor suspiciously.

"Loren," Officer Lewis spoke up, clearing his throat as he pointed to the living room wall, "you didn't happen to see who was responsible for all of this, did you?"

Mr. Thomas didn't answer for a moment; he simply stood there staring at the three of them with that pinched expression and those narrow, beady eyes. Finally, he stood up straighter and said, "I didn't see anyone, Officer." He paused and, taking a step closer, lowered his voice and said, "But it's not always easy to spot a ghost."

"Oh, good grief," Misty muttered, reaching up to rub her forehead.

"You're not still claiming this place is haunted, are you?" Officer Lewis asked skeptically.

"Miss Griffin wants to be left in peace," Mr. Thomas hissed, his eyes flashing as he pointed to the red paint on the wall. "Who else would leave such a message?" Turning back to face Misty, he pointed the same finger in her face and said, "Mark my words, young lady, if you don't leave this place, you'll regret it."

With that being said, Misty's old neighbor turned and shuffled from the room without another word, leaving the three of them to stare after him in silence.

"Officer Lewis," Misty said after Mr. Thomas was gone, "do you think *he* could have done this?"

"I doubt it. As eccentric as Loren is, he's quite harmless," Officer Lewis replied, reaching up to rub his bald head. "He used to work here, you know. He was the caretaker for about forty years and very committed to the Griffins. When her grandparents died and Loren retired, Cora gave him that cabin out in the woods."

Not entirely convinced, Misty crossed her arms and asked, "Who do you think it was, then?"

"I think it was probably just some kid having a bit of fun," Officer Lewis said with a shrug. "We rarely have crime in this area, Miss Raven, so I'm sure there's nothing to worry about."

Misty wasn't so sure about that, and after the two men left, she went around the house, locking all the windows and doors. She turned all the lights on, grabbed a hammer from her toolbox to use as a weapon, and spent the rest of the night scrubbing the ugly red message from her living room wall.

CHAPTER 4

When Saturday arrived, Misty was nervous about her outing with Adam. She'd always made a point not to make any strong attachments in the towns she visited, and she hoped Adam expected nothing more than friendship.

Adam arrived at exactly six o'clock, and Misty hurried out to meet him, nervously smoothing down her knee-length, khaki green dress.

"You look great," he greeted her with a warm smile as he opened the passenger side door.

"Thanks, so do you," she replied, watching as he circled around to the driver's door. He wore a button-up royal blue shirt that looked great with his dark complexion, he'd gotten a new haircut, and he smelled of fresh lemon and cedar. He was very handsome, and she suddenly found herself wondering if she should reconsider her decision about not making any strong attachments.

Adam took her to a small café in the center of town, and they sat outside under dozens of string lights and enjoyed the cool evening air.

"I heard about the incident at your house," Adam said after they'd placed their orders.

"Of course you did," Misty said with a chuckle.

Taking on a more serious tone, she asked, "Why do you think anyone would want me to leave? I only just got here, and hardly anyone even knows me."

"It seems that whoever it is doesn't want anyone living in that house," Adam replied with a shrug. Leaning his elbows onto the table, he said, "You need to be careful, Misty. It sounds like this could be a dangerous situation."

"Officer Lewis said I should get a gun, but since I can't stand the thought of shooting someone, I ordered some pepper spray instead," she replied with a sheepish laugh. A twinkle coming into her eyes, she added, "You know, I didn't realize there could be so much mystery in one small town."

"Oh, we have our fair share," Adam chuckled.

Something caught Adam's eye then, and he waved to someone over Misty's shoulder. "Misty," he said as a shadow fell over the table, "I'd like you to meet the owner of the café, Mr. Daniel Abraham."

Turning, Misty smiled up at the gentleman who appeared to be in his early forties, and offered her hand in greeting. "Mr. Abraham, it's nice to meet you. I'm Misty Raven."

"The new owner of the bed-and-breakfast," he said as more of a statement than a question.

"That's right," she nodded.

"I was good friends with Cora, you know," Mr. Abraham said. "She was a wonderful woman."

"Would you mind telling me a bit about her, Mr.

33

Abraham? I'd love to know more about the previous owner of my home."

Propping his hands on his hips, Mr. Abraham thought about the question for a moment before answering. Finally, he chuckled and said, "For one thing, she was fiercely independent. She was raised by her grandparents until she went to college, and when she got back with her business degree, she helped them run the bed-and-breakfast until they passed away. She was about twenty-four at the time and determined to make the best of it. She was friendly and well-liked, and everyone was devastated when she…when she died."

At those words, the light faded from Mr. Abraham's brown eyes, and he seemed relieved when one waiter stuck his head out of the front door and called to him. With a smile, he politely excused himself and walked away.

"What a nice man," Misty commented. "Does his wife work here, too?"

Adam reached for his glass of sweet tea and shook his head. "No, he never married."

"Is it strange that I want to know more about Cora Griffin?" Misty suddenly asked, pushing a stray curl away from her face. "I find it all to be a bit fascinating, while at the same time feeling terribly sorry for Cora and the fact that she died so young and tragically."

Adam shook his head. "I don't think it's strange at all. In fact, I'd say it's normal to want to know more about those who came before us, especially when there's also an air of mystery surrounding the situation."

The server brought their food then, and as Misty cut into her piece of baked chicken, she asked, "So, have you lived here all your life?"

"I sure have," Adam nodded. "I often travel to other nearby towns and cities for work, though. I'm actually going to Savannah next week for a few days. Have you ever been?"

"Yes, I have," Misty nodded, smiling. "It's one of the most beautiful places I've ever visited."

Savannah was only about thirty minutes away from Shady Pines and was the heart of the old south with its elaborate history, cobblestone streets, and magnificent live oaks. The city was drenched in southern charm, and Misty had nearly decided to settle there.

"I agree," Adam said, interrupting Misty's thoughts. "So, did you get a chance to visit our library?" When she nodded her head, he asked, "Did you find what you were looking for?"

The way he voiced the question immediately put Misty on guard, and she wondered if he somehow knew what she'd been searching for at the library.

"Not exactly," she replied with a tight smile. Clearing her throat, she added, "But if I remember correctly, you said that *you* would share some of the town's history with me."

"That's right, I did," he nodded. "What would you like to know?"

"Something interesting," she replied, choosing

her words carefully. "Something that you normally wouldn't share with visitors or newcomers."

Adam looked at her curiously for a moment before stating with a slight chuckle, "And here I thought you wanted to know about our founding fathers or what types of vegetables we grow."

"I *would* like to know those things, as well," she replied, smiling, "but after hearing the story of poor Cora Griffin, anything "normal" just seems boring in comparison."

Shaking his head, Adam laughed and said, "I see what you mean." Eyeing her for a moment, he added, "You're a unique individual, Misty Raven."

"Aren't we all?" Misty winked.

Once they'd finished their meal, Adam took Misty for a walk through the park. The night was peaceful and quiet, with crickets chirping among the rose bushes and a few random lightning bugs flashing among the trees, and Misty realized with a small sigh of relief that she was enjoying herself. It had been a long time since she'd gone out with a man, and she'd been afraid that it would be awkward.

After a moment of comfortable silence, Adam said, "Since I don't want to disappoint you with any boring stories of our small town, there *is* one tale the townspeople still murmur about that you may find interesting."

Tilting her head to look up at him through the darkness, Misty asked, "Oh? What's that?"

"About twenty-five years ago, several young women disappeared over the course of a year. They all left goodbye notes, but they've never been seen or heard from since."

Her brow furrowing, Misty asked, "Did the police investigate?"

"They did," Adam nodded, "but they couldn't find one single lead."

After a slight hesitation, Misty casually asked, "How old were the girls?"

"The first three were only seventeen, but the last one to disappear was a woman in her mid-twenties."

"What...what were their names?" Misty wanted to know.

Adam shrugged. "I can't remember. My mother knows much more about it than I do." Glancing down at Misty, he smiled and said, "I'll have to introduce the two of you soon, and maybe she can tell you more."

"I'd like that," Misty said with a small smile of her own.

As they turned to make their way back to Adam's car, Misty reached up to touch her locket and softly asked, "Do you think the disappearance of those women could somehow be connected to Cora Griffin's death?"

"I don't think so," Adam replied. "Everyone always thought that Cora's death resulted from a lover's quarrel, so I doubt the two are connected. Plus, both incidents happened over ten years apart."

"I see," Misty murmured. Bumping Adam with her elbow, she added playfully, "This town certainly has an interesting history, and now I'm getting threatening messages left on my wall. Maybe it wasn't such a good idea to move here after all."

"Come on, we're not that bad," Adam chuckled. "Besides, we haven't had anything exciting happen around here in years, so I'd say you've shaken things up a bit."

When they arrived back at the car, Adam opened the door for Misty and said warmly, "And just for the record, I think it *was* a good idea for you to move here."

That night, after Adam dropped Misty off at her house, she stayed up well past midnight and worked in the master bedroom, thinking over everything he'd told her. Thankfully, he hadn't seemed too suspicious over her prying questions, and she had the feeling she just might be getting closer to the truth.

The clock had just struck half-past twelve when Misty found a small box pushed against the back of the top shelf of the master bedroom closet. Her eyes alight with interest, she grabbed a step ladder and pulled the box down, blowing the dust off the top before opening it. Inside, Misty found some old pictures of who she assumed were Cora and her grandparents. She then found a photo of Cora and a young man; Cora was leaning against him, her smile bright as she held up her hand to reveal an engagement ring.

"So, that's Hank Johnson," Misty murmured.

The two made a lovely couple. Cora was tall and slim, with wavy brown hair that hung loosely around her shoulders, and Hank was quite handsome with striking blue eyes and a charming smile. They looked so happy that Misty couldn't help wondering what had happened to them.

As she moved to put the box away, she realized there was a small card tucked into the corner that she'd overlooked. Pulling it out, Misty realized it was a florist card, and written on the small white piece of paper were the words, *"Cora, please forgive me for everything. I love you so much, and I don't want to lose you. I'm coming to see you tonight in the hope that we can talk things out. Love, -H."*

Written beneath his note in slanted, feminine handwriting was, "Yes!!!" with several hearts drawn all around. Misty then noticed the date, and her brow furrowed when she realized it was the day Cora died. If she and Hank were going to talk things out, why had she killed herself? It seemed they loved each other a great deal and were both eager to renew their relationship.

It made little sense, and as Misty put everything into the box and placed it back on the shelf, she couldn't help the niggling thought in the back of her mind that something wasn't right.

CHAPTER 5

The next day, Misty drove into town to do a bit of shopping at the local farmer's market. It was held in the park every other weekend, and Misty was surprised to see so many vendors. There were rows upon rows of booths and trucks filled with fruit, vegetables, flowers, baked goods, jams, jellies, and even a few handcrafted items. Before she realized it, she'd spent over two hours browsing and buying, and she'd just come to stand at a booth filled with homemade cookies and cakes when she heard a familiar voice speak out from behind.

"If you want my opinion, you should go for the pecan pie brownies; they're to die for."

Turning, Misty found a smiling Tori standing there holding a basket filled with fruit, fresh spices, and a glass of peach tea in her other hand.

"Tori, it's nice to see you again," Misty greeted her. Turning to point at the pecan pie brownies, she asked, "So, these are the best?"

"Well, actually everything is amazing, but those brownies are my favorite." When Misty glanced at her quizzically, she added with a laugh, "This is my mom's booth so I may be a little bias, but she's an excellent baker."

Just then, Tori's mother stepped up to the booth

carrying an extra tray of desserts, and Tori immediately introduced the two women. Tori's mom, Mrs. Amy, was a lovely woman, and it was clear to see where Tori's sparkling blue eyes, strawberry blonde hair, and bright, friendly smile came from.

By the time the three women finished chatting, Misty's arms were tired and cramped from holding all of her purchases, and Tori graciously offered to help carry her things to her car.

"I heard what happened to your house the other night," Tori said as they walked across the park. "You know, if you're interested in getting a dog, I help run our local pet shelter and I'd be happy to introduce you to some of our loveable canine residents."

"I've actually never had a dog before, but I've always wanted one," Misty said, shifting one basket against her hip. "I can't have one right now with all the renovations, but maybe I can get one once I'm finished."

Tori glanced at her and said, "You could keep the dog outside, you know. It could guard your property."

"Oh, no," Misty shook her head, laughing. "If I had a pet, it would be inside sleeping by my bed every night."

As they neared the last booth, Tori nodded at the two men who were gathering up their things to leave.

"Going home so soon?" Tori asked, stopping to

chat with them for a moment.

"I'm afraid so," the younger man said. "We didn't do so great today."

"I told him there was no need to come today," the older man snapped, his eyes flashing. "Craig can barely sell any of his woodwork with all of these new vendors selling baked goods and such. People are so busy buying cakes and cookies that they don't want to spend any more money at Craig's booth."

People don't want to spend their money because the prices on this stuff are outrageous, Misty thought, trying to keep her expression neutral.

Her cheeks flushing at the obvious remark against her mother, Tori cleared her throat and said, "That's too bad. Oh, have y'all met Misty? She recently bought the old bed-and-breakfast. Misty, this is Rick Harley and his brother, Craig. Rick is a plumber."

Her eyes lighting up, Misty smiled at Rick and said, "That's good to know, because I'll be needing a plumber soon. Could you possibly come by sometime next week to give me a quote?"

"I won't be able to come by until Thursday," he stated matter-of-factly.

"That will be perfect," Misty replied with a nod. "Do you have a business card?"

Reaching into his pocket, Rick withdrew a card and handed it to Misty without uttering another word. He then picked up a box of Craig's things

42

and stalked away, leaving the three behind to watch in silence.

"I apologize for his rude behavior," Craig finally said, his face red with embarrassment as he stepped forward to shake Misty's hand. With a warm smile, he added, "It's nice to meet you, Misty. Welcome to Shady Pines."

Craig was a bit taller than the two women, with broad shoulders and tanned, strong hands. He seemed to be much more friendly than his brother, and Misty didn't miss the way he looked at Tori.

"I'll see you at the harvest party, won't I?" He asked Tori.

"I'm sure you'll see me before then, Craig," Tori stated playfully.

As the two continued on their way to Misty's car, she glanced at Tori and said, "It seems you have an admirer."

Blinking in surprise, Tori's cheeks flushed, and she said, "Who, Craig? No way; he's in his mid-thirties and at least ten years older than me."

Her lips twitching, Misty shrugged and said, "Whatever you say."

Once everything was loaded into her car, Misty touched Tori's arm and said, "Thank you so much for your help, Tori, that was very kind of you."

"You'll learn soon enough that helping out is something people in small towns do quite well," she replied with a grin. "I'll see you soon, okay?"

Misty nodded and waved goodbye to her new friend, a smile on her face as she climbed into her car. She'd never had many friends and hadn't intended on making any in Shady Pines, but she was quickly discovering that was proving to be impossible in this town.

The next morning arrived with a gloriously cool breeze in tow, and Misty decided to work outside and enjoy the nice weather for a change. She started in on the overgrown shrubs first, and by the time noon rolled around, she'd managed to clear the entire area around the front of the house. She'd just taken a step back to survey how much nicer the house already looked when she heard the sound of a vehicle approaching. Turning, she saw a large white truck with "Barlow Hardware" written along the side pulling into her front yard.

"Afternoon," Brice called out with a friendly wave. He climbed from the truck and went around to the back to pull out a few buckets of paint from the truck bed. "I thought I'd bring out that extra paint you ordered," he said as he came to stand beside Misty. Taking in all the work she'd done, he whistled and said, "You did this all by yourself?"

Nodding, Misty took one of the buckets and said, "I certainly did."

As they carried the paint around to the back porch, Brice questioned, "Why didn't you ask someone to come out and help you with these shrubs? That's a lot of hard work."

"I'm used to hard work," she stated, sitting her load on the porch floor. "Thank you for delivering the paint, by the way, but I could have come into town and picked it up."

"You don't like the thought of anyone helping you out, do you?" Brice asked, cocking one eyebrow in the air as he leaned against the porch banister and studied her.

"Tori helped me carry my baskets to the car yesterday, and I didn't mind at all," she replied tartly. Crossing her arms, she added with a shrug, "I'm just used to doing things on my own, I guess."

"Don't you have a family to help you?"

Kicking a small rock from the porch with the toe of her boot, Misty shook her head and replied, "No, I was raised in the foster system."

Brice blinked in surprise, his dark blue eyes instantly filling with sympathy. "I'm sorry, Misty. That had to be tough."

Wishing to take the subject from herself, Misty asked, "What about you? Do your parents live here?"

"My dad died when I was sixteen, and my mom remarried about five years ago and is now living in North Carolina," Brice replied. "So, it's just me and Pops, and a few aunts, uncles, and cousins."

"I'm sorry about your father," Misty said softly. "You're lucky to have your grandfather, though; you two seem to work well together."

"Oh yeah," Brice nodded. "He's the best. I

started working at the store right after Dad died, and one day it'll be mine."

"I'm sure it's nice to have a future that's secure and settled," Misty stated, her voice a bit wistful. Her future had always been uncertain, and she'd never been blessed to have the guidance or support of a family. She'd often imagined, however, what it would be like to know what you want to do with the rest of your life and that you'll always be surrounded by those you love. When she was little, she'd dreamed of it every night, but the older she got, the more she realized that one doesn't always get what one wishes for.

"You could have a future here," Brice stated, and Misty glanced at him quizzically. "Shady Pines is a great place to settle down, and once people get to know you, you'll see how it feels to have an entire town for a family. You could keep this place and turn it back into a bed-and-breakfast."

"I don't know," Misty shrugged. "We'll see."

Brice said nothing for a moment, but the silence didn't bother Misty as she moved the paint buckets to the far corner where the rest of her supplies rested. She liked to keep everything neat and organized; that was one part of her life that she could control.

"Well, young lady," Brice finally said, slapping his thigh as he stood up straight and began rolling up his sleeves, "if we want to get the rest of these shrubs cleaned up by nightfall, we'd better get to it."

"What are you doing?" Misty asked, her eyes wide as she watched Brice pick up a nearby shovel.

"I'm going to dig this thing up," he replied, pointing to a thorny, overgrown holly bush. "It's too close to the back steps. Wouldn't you prefer to plant an azalea bush or something less prickly here?"

"You really don't have to help me, Brice," Misty told him as she took a quick sip of water and hurried down the steps to join him.

"That's what friends are for," he said with a wink, just before digging the shovel into the ground with his foot. "You're not afraid to have friends, are you? Or to accept their help?"

Sighing, Misty's lips twitched as she shook her head and said, "No, I'm not afraid." Stepping closer, she touched him on the sleeve and said sincerely, "Thank you, Brice."

The two worked tirelessly until the sky was filled with brilliant bursts of orange and gold as the sun made its final descent for the day. Although Misty didn't like to admit that she ever needed anyone, as she'd always just had herself to rely on, she was grateful for Brice's help, and his company seemed to make the time go by faster. The work was hard, but they had a good time together, and as the day slowly started turning to night, there was only one last bush to dig up and they would be finished.

"This bush looks like it was here with the dinosaurs," Brice said, huffing as he forced the shovel through the hardened ground. Misty did the

47

same with her shovel on the other side, and it wasn't long before the old bush began losing its firm grip on the earth.

Through the growing shadows, Misty thought she caught sight of something other than dirt and roots in the ground, and she bent down to take a closer look.

"Brice, what is this?" She asked, beckoning to him with her hand. He kneeled beside her, and she pointed to the hole she'd just dug.

She watched as he bent closer, moving the dirt away from the object with his fingers, and when a look of alarm lit upon his face, she knew her suspicions were correct.

Beneath the shrubs by the back porch were the skeletal remains of a human body.

Both Brice and Misty jumped away, their eyes wide with horror. Clutching Brice's arm, Misty said hoarsely, "I think we'd better call the police." Looking up at him, she added in a low tone, "If my guess is correct, this is the body of Hank Johnson, Cora Griffin's fiancé.

CHAPTER 6

Misty had only been in town for a little over a week, and this was already the second visit she'd received from the police. Finding a message written on your living room wall and a body buried in your backyard wasn't normal, and Misty was anxious to find answers. Officer Lewis, however, seemed less than enthusiastic.

"We'll have to get the coroner to check dental records and such to see if this really is Hank Johnson," he said once his team had bagged the body and rolled it to an awaiting vehicle.

"What then?" Misty wanted to know.

"Well, it's too late to do much right now, but I'll come back out tomorrow when it's light and check around the burial site to make certain we didn't miss anything." Officer Lewis was walking around to the front of the house as he spoke, and when he suddenly stopped to point a finger at Misty, she skidded to a halt, barely able to keep from running right into him. "I want you to leave the site completely alone until we're finished. Is that understood? I don't want the area tampered with; there could still be evidence, although it's highly unlikely after all this time."

"Yes, sir," she nodded in agreement. Officer

Lewis continued walking, and she hurried after him. "What happens if you don't find any evidence? How will you catch the person responsible?"

"I doubt whoever killed Hank Johnson is still hanging around town, Miss Raven," Officer Lewis stated with a slight snicker. "That was fifteen years ago, and I'm thinking that Cora killed him before she killed herself."

"I don't agree, Officer," Misty said, proceeding to tell him about the pictures and note from the florist she'd found. "It seems to me they truly were in love and planned on getting back together. I think they were both murdered."

With a sigh, Officer Lewis looked at Misty and said somewhat impatiently, "Miss Raven, don't be ridiculous, and please don't attempt to do my job for me. I'm a trained police officer, so I think I should know what I'm doing."

Her cheeks flushing, Misty nodded and stepped away, taking the hint loud and clear. Officer Lewis didn't care to hear her opinion, and that was fine…it didn't stop her from still having one, though.

"You okay?" Brice asked as he stepped up beside her. He'd been talking to one of the other officers, and Misty was suddenly glad he'd decided to stick around today. Otherwise, she would have discovered the body all by herself.

"Yes, just shocked that this is happening," she replied with a sigh. Turning to look at him, she asked, "Do you think this is why that message was written on my wall? Someone knew that body was buried outside, and they didn't want me to find it?"

Pursing his lips in thought, Brice finally shook his head, his eyes filling with worry as he said in a low tone, "If that's the case, Misty, then the murderer is still here, living in this town."

Her eyes widening, Misty clutched Brice's arm and said, "Brice, that means it could be someone you've known your whole life. Maybe even someone you see every day."

"This is crazy," he sighed, running his fingers through his hair. "I can't believe anyone in this town could be a murderer."

Reaching up to touch her locket, Misty said softly, "Sometimes you don't know a person as well as you think."

When Officer Lewis arrived the next morning, Misty was outside waiting for him. She watched from the back porch as he made a thorough investigation of the area where the body was found, and it was all she could do not to join him in his search.

"Find anything?" She asked when he stopped to inspect something stuck in the soil.

"No," he finally replied with a sigh. "Just a rock."

Pursing her lips in disappointment, Misty

continued to watch in silence. After a moment, she asked, "Officer Lewis, were you here when the disappearances of those women occurred twenty-five years ago?"

Glancing up at Misty in surprise, he said, "Yes, I was. I'd actually just joined the force when the first girl disappeared."

Twiddling her thumbs, Misty commented, "It's very strange; Adam was telling me about it. What do you think happened to them?"

"I think they got enough of small town living and ran off," he replied with a huff as he dug his hand shovel a bit deeper.

"*All* of them?" Misty questioned in disbelief. "Wouldn't they have told someone? Or at least contacted their families by now?"

"They were all good friends," Officer Lewis replied with a shrug, reaching up to wipe the sweat from his forehead. "I think they planned the whole thing."

"What…what about the older woman?"

"She was their Spanish teacher." Stopping, Officer Lewis looked up at Misty with a furrowed brow and asked, "Why are you asking so many questions about something that happened twenty-five years ago?"

"Just trying to make conversation," she stated casually. "I thought it sounded like an interesting story."

"Well, it's over and done with, and I think we should let the past stay where it is."

With a sigh, Misty sat on the porch banister and didn't say another word. About twenty minutes later, Officer Lewis stood up and said, "There's nothing more to be found here. You can cover the hole back over now if you want, Miss Raven; my work here is done."

Following him around the house to his car, Misty asked, "Will you let me know when you find out if the dead body really is Mr. Johnson?"

"I won't have to, Miss Raven; the whole town will know about it," he replied, nodding goodbye as he climbed into his car and drove away.

Two days later, Misty discovered that Officer Lewis was right. She'd gone into town to buy a new pair of work boots and stopped in at Tori's coffee shop for a pumpkin spice latte. As soon as she stepped inside, the buzz of excited chatter met her ears.

"Did someone win the lottery?" Misty asked when she pushed her way to the counter.

"Haven't you heard?" Tori asked, her eyes wide. When Misty shook her head, she leaned closer and said, "The body you found really *is* Hank Johnson. You were right, Misty!"

"What are the police going to do now?" Misty asked.

"I don't know," Tori shrugged. "Officer Lewis said there wasn't much they *could* do."

"Nonsense," Misty declared emphatically. "They could start questioning people who were around at the time. Does Mr. Johnson's family still live in the area?"

"Yes, his mother does," Tori nodded. With a light coming into her eyes, she pointed to a box filled with cookies and said, "I was actually about to take this over to her house to share my condolences. Would you like to join me?"

Hesitating, Misty thought the question over for a moment. She knew Tori was just as curious as she was to find out who killed Hank Johnson and Cora Griffin, but was it really their place to interfere with a police investigation?

On the other hand, Misty felt a strange, overwhelming need to help solve this mystery. The house belonged to her now, after all, and she was responsible for discovering the body of Cora's fiancé. She knew that Officer Lewis wasn't going to put much effort into the matter, and Misty felt that she somehow owed it to Cora to find the truth. She may not have ever known the previous owner of her home, but she felt a connection with her nonetheless and wanted to do what she could to help find Cora's killer.

"What are we waiting for?" Misty finally replied, a twinkle coming into her own eyes. "Let's go."

The drive to Hank Johnson's family home was a short one, and Misty let Tori lead the way as they walked up to the front door and knocked. The door was opened by a woman in her mid-sixties, and Misty's heart immediately went out to her when she saw her red-rimmed eyes and the handkerchief she clutched in her hand.

"Mrs. Johnson, I just wanted to stop by and offer my condolences," Tori said, reaching out to squeeze the older woman's hand. "I'm so sorry about your son. I brought these cookies along; I know they're your favorite."

With a tear-filled smile, Mrs. Johnson said, "Thank you, dear. This is so kind. Would you and your friend like to come in for some tea? I could use the company."

As Mrs. Johnson led the two women into the living room, Tori made the introductions. When Mrs. Johnson realized Misty was the one who found her son, her eyes widened and she reached out to take Misty's hand.

"Thank you so much, Miss Raven," she said, her voice trembling. "I've spent the last fifteen years wondering whatever happened to my son, and even though my heart is broken, it's a relief to know what happened to him."

Her heart clenching with sympathy, Misty nodded and said gently, "I'm very sorry for your loss, Mrs. Johnson."

After Mrs. Johnson brought them all a glass of tea, they sat down and began to chat. Misty's eyes wandered all around the room, taking in the many photographs of Mrs. Johnson, Hank, and a man she assumed to be Hank's father.

Pretending she didn't know what Hank looked like, Misty pointed to one of the photos and asked, "Is that your son?"

"Oh, yes, that's my Hank," she said, smiling softly as she picked up the photo. She touched the cool glass that encased the picture and sighed, the pain in her eyes moving Misty to tears. "He was such a good boy," she added softly, "always working hard and helping others. He looked so much like his father, God rest both of their souls. I've truly been lost without them."

"Mrs. Johnson, I don't wish to pry, but do you have any idea who would have wanted to kill your son?" Misty asked in a gentle tone.

Sighing, Mrs. Johnson shook her head and said, "I don't have the faintest idea; everyone loved Hank."

"Do you know why he and Cora broke up?" Tori spoke up.

"No, he said he didn't want to talk about it," Mrs. Johnson replied, turning to replace the photo on the table by the sofa. "Cora was a sweet girl; I never understood what happened between them."

"Cora Griffin was a flirt, Amelia Johnson, and you know it."

They all turned in surprise to find a redheaded woman around Mrs. Johnson's age emerging from the foyer, a casserole dish in her hand.

"The front door was unlocked," she stated matter-of-factly, "so I let myself in."

"That's alright, Sandra, you can put that

casserole in the kitchen," Mrs. Johnson told the woman. Turning to look at Misty, she said, "Sandra Neely is one of my neighbors; we've known each other our whole lives."

When Mrs. Neely returned, Mrs. Johnson introduced her to Misty, but before Misty couldn't even utter a "nice to meet you", the other woman pursed her lips and said, "What are you girls doing over here bothering Amelia during such a trying time? She needs to be resting."

"We just came by to offer our condolences, Mrs. Neely," Tori explained.

Cocking a red, manicured eyebrow, Mrs. Neely stated pointedly, "Well, I don't believe that should take all afternoon."

"Mrs. Neely," Misty spoke up before the woman ran them out, "why did you say that Cora Griffin was a flirt?"

"Because it's the truth," she snapped, her green eyes flashing. "She dated half the men in this town, the hussy."

"Sandra, just because she broke things off with your son doesn't make her a hussy," Mrs. Johnson sighed.

Her eyes brightening, Misty sat up straighter and asked, "Cora dated your son, Mrs. Neely?"

"She most certainly did," Mrs. Neely sniffed. "She broke poor Jeremy's heart."

"It wasn't *her* fault that she didn't love Jeremy," Mrs. Johnson stated with a scowl.

Rising to her full height, Mrs. Neely looked

down her nose at her neighbor and huffed. "All I'm saying is that she led him on, right along with several other young men in this town, including your Hank. After all, *she's* the one that broke off their engagement, and for all we know, she's the one who killed him."

With that being said, Mrs. Neely spun on her heel and marched from the house, her head held high.

After a moment of awkward silence, Mrs. Johnson finally said, "That Sandra always *was* too outspoken." Glancing apologetically at her two visitors, she added, "I'm sorry for her behavior."

Misty and Tori stayed a bit longer and chatted with Mrs. Johnson, and as they were leaving, Misty asked one last question.

"Mrs. Johnson, who were some of the other men Cora dated? If you don't mind my asking."

"Hmm, let me see," Mrs. Johnson replied, tapping her chin. "I believe she dated Daniel Abraham, Rick Harley, and…there was one more, but I can't remember his name."

"Rick Harley?" Tori asked in surprise. "Craig's brother?"

Mrs. Johnson nodded. "Yes, that's right."

The two women said their goodbyes, and as they walked to Tori's car, Misty said, "How can we find out who the other man was that Cora dated?"

Tori thought about it for a moment, her eyes lighting up when an idea struck her. "We can ask Mom; she'll know. I'll ask her tomorrow night when I go over to her and dad's house for supper. Hey, would you like to join us?"

Surprised at the kind invitation, as Misty wasn't used to such gestures, she simply smiled and nodded her head in agreement. Being shuffled around in the foster system had never given her the opportunity to make many friends, and as she became older, she'd become more and more reclusive. There was something different about this place, though, and Misty found herself finally starting to come out of her shell a bit. She had to make certain, though, not to get distracted from her original purpose for coming here.

CHAPTER 7

The next morning, Rick Harley came by to give Misty a quote for the plumbing work that needed to be done. He was only a bit nicer than when she'd seen him at the farmer's market, but not much. He seemed to keep a permanent scowl on his face, and Misty got the feeling he didn't like being at the house.

"It's been a long time since I've been out here," he muttered, almost to himself, as they walked inside.

Not wishing to miss the opportunity, Misty said, "I heard that you and Cora Griffin dated for a bit."

The scowl growing worse, Rick said in a steely tone, "Only for a few months, and then she dumped me for Hank."

The way he said Hank's name let Misty know he didn't think too highly of Cora's fiancé…or ex-fiancé, whichever it was, and with a heartfelt sigh, Misty said, "It's so sad what happened to them."

Cutting her eyes up and to the side, Misty watched Rick's face closely for any sign of emotion. When his only response was, "what work do you need to be done?", Misty had to force back a sigh of frustration.

After showing him all the toilets, bathtubs, and sinks that would need replacing, Misty showed him back out, and he said he would get a quote together within the next day or so.

"It's not a rush," Misty said, smiling politely. Clearing her throat, she asked, "Do you and Mrs. Harley have children? I'm afraid I don't know much about the people in this town yet, so I'm having to ask all sorts of nosy questions."

She ended her sentence with a sheepish laugh, and Rick simply pursed his lips and said, "No, we don't have any children. Good day, Miss Raven."

As Misty stood in the doorway watching him leave, she wondered what Cora ever saw in him. Perhaps he used to be different. Perhaps he changed when Cora died...or when she "dumped" him for Hank. He seemed so uptight and bitter; like he hated life and everyone in it. Misty wondered how on earth his wife lived with him and immediately felt sorry for the woman she'd never met.

That night, Tori came by the house to pick Misty up for supper, as she felt it would be too difficult for Misty to find her parents' house by herself.

"They live down a long dirt road that isn't anywhere to be found on a map," she'd said with a laugh, "so I'll just pick you up a few minutes before six."

As they drove to the Barlow home, Misty quickly realized how true Tori's statement was. After traveling several miles from town, they turned down a series of dirt roads before finally arriving at a beautiful farm filled with sprawling acres of green grass, wooden fences, and a two-story white farmhouse.

"This is where you grew up?" Misty asked, her eyes wide as she took it all in.

"Yes, it is," Tori replied with a smile. "My parents raise horses."

When they pulled up in front of the house, Misty was surprised to see that Brice and his grandfather were there as well.

"They come by and eat with us all the time," Tori commented as she led Misty into the house.

"Misty, it's so good to see you again," Tori's mother, Mrs. Amy, greeted Misty when they walked inside, pulling her into a warm hug. Turning to motion to her husband, Neil, who was a bear of a man with thinning brown hair and a wide smile, she introduced the two of them.

"So, this is the troublemaker Brice and Tori have been telling me about," Mr. Neil said as he shook Misty's hand, a mischievous glint in his eye.

"I've said no such thing, Misty. Don't pay him any attention," Tori called out from the dining room as she set the table.

Brice stepped up beside Misty and crossed his arms, grinning at her as he said, "I, on the other hand, might have said such a thing."

"Why does that not surprise me?" Misty cocked an eyebrow at him.

Within a few moments, everyone sat down to eat the delicious meal of chili and cornbread Mrs. Amy prepared, and Misty sat quietly for a bit, listening as everyone around her talked and laughed. Here was the perfect example of a family, one that Misty had never truly seen for herself. Her foster families had quite often been large, but they'd never sat down together to eat or talk or share things; they'd simply lived their own lives and tried to stay out of each other's way. As Misty watched the camaraderie and familiarity that comes with a close-knit family, she realized just how much she'd missed growing up.

"Mom," Tori spoke up, glancing over at Misty, "do you remember who Cora Griffin dated? Mrs. Johnson told Misty and me about Jeremy Neely, Daniel Abraham, and Rick Harley, but there was one more that she couldn't remember."

"Hmm, let me see," Mrs. Amy said, sitting her spoon down as she tapped her chin in thought. "She was much younger than me, but I do remember that she dated those three you just mentioned. I can't seem to remember a fourth man, though. Can you, Neil?"

Mr. Neil shook his head. "No, I don't either."

"How is Mrs. Johnson doing?" Mr. Barlow, or "Pop" as Tori and Brice so fondly called him, spoke up.

"She's heartbroken, of course, but relieved to know what happened to her son," Tori replied as she reached for another piece of cornbread.

The conversation drifted a bit and, gathering her nerve, Misty cleared her throat and said, "Mrs. Amy, I heard that a few women disappeared from the town about twenty-five years ago. Do you remember that?"

"Oh my, yes," Mrs. Amy nodded, reaching up to push a stray tendril of her graying strawberry blonde hair behind one ear. "That was a strange time. I believe three of the girls were about seventeen, and their teacher was around my age. They never knew what happened to them. I heard that the younger girls left behind a goodbye note, but I find it hard to believe that they abandoned their home and families and have never come back or at least called to let their parents know they're alive and well."

"Do you remember any of their names?"

Brice glanced at Misty curiously when she voiced the question, but Misty ignored him.

"The three girls were Jessica Hendricks, Tabitha O'Reilly, and Stephanie Ruis," Mrs. Amy replied as she refilled her husband's chili bowl. Sitting back down, she pursed her lips and said, "As for the teacher's name…oh, what was it…goodness, I don't know what has happened to my memory."

"It starts going around the age of fifty," Pop stated, and they all laughed.

Looking at Misty, Mrs. Amy said apologetically, "I can't remember her name, honey. I'm sorry. All I remember is that she was from Mexico or South America or somewhere like that, and she had one of those foreign-sounding names."

"She wasn't from here?" Brice asked.

Mrs. Amy shook her head. "No, she and her

husband moved to town when he got stationed at the army base near here, and she started teaching at the school. I was expecting Tori at the time and suffering from a horrible case of preeclampsia, so I wasn't making many social calls, but she seemed like a nice person. After the three girls went missing, it wasn't long before she disappeared, too."

"What about her husband?" Tori questioned.

"From what I can recall, he got shipped overseas a couple of weeks before she disappeared," Mrs. Amy explained. "We never saw him again either."

"Did they have any children?" Misty asked.

"Not that I know of, but as I said, I was pretty much out of the loop during that time," Mrs. Amy replied.

Pop asked what was for dessert then, and the conversation immediately shifted. Misty helped Tori and Mrs. Amy clear the table, and then they all enjoyed a slice of homemade, seven layer chocolate cake.

"I can understand why you do so well at the farmer's market, Mrs. Amy," Misty told her. "This cake is amazing, and those pecan pie brownies I bought the other day were heavenly."

"Oh, thank you," Mrs. Amy beamed at the compliment.

Once everyone was finished eating, Brice asked Misty if she'd like to take a walk with him.

"Uncle Neil just bought a new horse, and I'd love for you to see him," he told her.

Misty agreed, her step light as they went outside and headed for the barn. She'd always wanted a horse when she was young and was excited to see so many at one time.

Brice opened the large barn door, and the two stepped inside. The area before them stretched out into a long, open walkway with stalls lining either side, and Misty stopped for a moment to look at all the beautiful horses poking their heads out.

"Oh, they're all so beautiful," she breathed, stepping over to the nearest horse to rub its muzzle gently. The massive creature smelled her hand for a moment and then nudged her fingers, as if expecting a treat to appear.

"This handsome fella is a Paint, and his name is Little Joe," Brice explained as he reached out to rub the horse's nose.

"As in Little Joe Cartwright?" Misty asked, tilting her head to look up at Brice.

Raising his eyebrows in surprise, Brice asked, "You've seen Bonanza?"

"I certainly have," she replied with a smile. "I had a huge crush on Little Joe when I was young…" pausing, a glint came into her eyes and she added with a wink, "I actually still do."

Laughing, Brice led Misty down to another stall, and when she saw the magnificent Appaloosa for the first time, she gasped in awe. The horse stood a proud sixteen hands tall, and his coat was a light brown that faded into a white rump with black spots. His mane and tail were a shiny black, and he had a splash of white going across his face. He was breathtaking, and Misty simply leaned against the stall door for a moment, staring at him.

"Misty, I'd like for you to meet…"

"If you say Wooster, I'll never speak to you again," she interrupted, a grin pulling at her lips as she beckoned to the horse.

"Oh, no, he's much too regal to be named Wooster," Brice replied, a smile in his voice. Clearing his throat, he stated, "This is Trampas."

Bursting into laughter, Misty turned to look at Brice and said, "Apparently, someone around here likes old Westerns."

Grinning, Brice nodded and said, "Uncle Neil is to blame for that. Isn't it great? Aunt Amy hates it."

They continued to walk, observing all the horses and discussing how the farm was run, and they soon found themselves back outside. As the sun was setting, creating a breathtaking scene over the rolling fields of green grass and white picket fences, Misty breathed a sigh of contentment. She'd never settled down anywhere before, but it wouldn't take much effort to get used to this place.

"So, I'm curious about something," Brice spoke up as they made their way back up to the house. When Misty glanced over at him questioningly, he asked, "Why are you so curious about the disappearance of those four women?"

Caught off guard, Misty blinked, barely keeping herself from tripping over a small rock in her path.

"Oh, well…" she hesitated, shrugging as she said, "it just seems like an interesting story, I guess. Few small towns have such a fascinating history."

"Women disappearing over twenty-five years ago is fascinating?" Brice raised his eyebrows. When Misty didn't respond, he stopped walking and took her arm, forcing her to stop as well. Studying her closely, he said, "You can trust me, Misty. I hope you know that."

Misty tried to maintain a neutral expression but failed, and finally she said with a sigh, "Thank you, Brice. Maybe…maybe someday I can explain everything."

"I'd like that," he said, his gaze warm and his hand still holding her arm.

Clearing her throat awkwardly, Misty pulled away and began walking again, suddenly feeling the need to create some space between them. He'd said she could trust him, but Misty didn't trust easily. She'd been misled and misguided many times in her life, and she wasn't ready to let her guard down just yet.

CHAPTER 8

Early the next morning, Misty decided to go for a walk. She wanted to explore more of her property, and also find Mr. Thomas's cabin. She hadn't seen him since her home was broken in to and had wondered at his whereabouts.

The morning was overcast and foggy, and a light mist hovered above the ground as several crows cawed loudly from the treetops. Misty found a small, overgrown path that wound deep into the woods, and as she entered the shadowy abyss and began to follow the path, she pulled her sweater tighter around her shoulders. She hadn't realized how dark and desolate the woods could be, and the way the bushes continuously rustled and a layer of fog hung around the tops of the trees made it seem almost like a haunted forest.

Don't let your imagination run away with you, she told herself, her eyes searching the dark trees for any signs of life.

After nearly ten minutes of walking, Misty stumbled upon a small clearing with a cabin she assumed to belong to Mr. Thomas. As she drew closer, she noticed a driveway on the opposite side of the house that must lead out to the road. She knew her neighbor wouldn't appreciate the intrusion, but she marched up to the door, nonetheless, and knocked. When no one answered, she slowly pushed open the door and poked her head inside.

"Mr. Thomas?" she called out, but there was no answer.

Glancing around uncertainly, Misty stepped inside and slowly surveyed the small cabin. The living room stretched out before her, with an old recliner resting before a small TV, and the kitchen was to her right. She could see a bedroom just beyond the kitchen, and as she stepped further into the living room, her eyes fell upon a framed photograph resting on a nearby desk. Walking closer, Misty realized the picture was of Cora and her grandparents, and when her gaze drifted downward, she noticed some old newspaper clippings.

Looking over her shoulder to make certain Mr. Thomas wasn't lurking in the corner watching, Misty picked up the clippings and read them. One set that was paper-clipped together appeared to be their obituaries, while the other was a small article written about Cora's death. Her brow furrowing, Misty wondered why Mr. Thomas would have saved all of this.

Suddenly, Misty heard a sound coming from the back of the house, and she quickly replaced the clippings and hurried back outside, quietly shutting the cabin door behind her. Feeling a little nervous and on edge, she decided to return home.

As Misty made her way back to the house, she

noticed the woods seemed even darker than before and wondered if perhaps it was going to rain. The air also seemed cooler, and Misty rubbed her arms, fighting off a chill. Just then, a sudden, forceful breeze rustled the branches overhead and sent leaves and pine needles falling all along the path. The birds no longer chirped and even the crows were quiet, and Misty found herself feeling a bit anxious to be out of these woods.

Suddenly, the sound of crunching leaves and snapping twigs made its way to Misty's ears, and she paused, listening. *That's strange,* she thought when the noise stopped, and shaking off the feeling that she was being followed, she continued on her way, her steps quicker this time.

There it was again. Spinning around to the right, Misty peered through the thick trees, squinting as she tried to see who or what was out there. Could it be a deer or rabbit? Or perhaps a human?

"Mr. Thomas?" Misty called out, her voice trembling a bit. "Is that you?"

When she received only silence as a response, Misty swallowed past the lump in her throat and turned to hurry on her way. Perhaps she was imagining things; perhaps the sound was only an echo of her own footsteps. But when Misty suddenly heard the pounding of running feet along the forest floor, her heart leaped into her throat and she began running, too. Tree branches and bushes reached out to grab at her as she ran along the path, her breathing heavy and the racing of her heart loud as it pounded in her ears. Was she overreacting? She wasn't sure; all she knew was that she needed to get out of here as quickly as possible. Something…or someone…seemed to be chasing her, and she didn't think their intentions were friendly.

Finally, after what seemed like an eternity, Misty broke through the woods into the clearing of her backyard, and she stopped for a moment to catch her breath. Turning to look over her shoulder, she didn't see anyone or anything, nor did she hear the footsteps any longer. ***It must have been a deer,*** Misty thought. Feeling a little silly, she brushed the hair out of her face and slowly walked up to the house, her legs weak and trembling from the run.

She'd just made it to the back porch steps when she heard the sound of a car door closing. Walking around the side of the house, Misty saw Craig Harley climbing onto her front porch, a box in his hand.

"Craig, how are you?" she called out, a smile on her face as she approached.

Looking a bit startled, Craig turned to see Misty and said, "Oh, hello, Misty. I…I'm sorry for just popping by like this. I hope it's okay?"

"Of course," she replied, opening the front door and beckoning him to come inside. "Would you like some coffee?"

Craig readily agreed, and as the two walked into the kitchen, Misty took off her sweater and said,

"Please excuse my appearance; I went for a walk in the woods this morning."

While Misty put on a pot of coffee, Craig opened the box he carried and said, "I wanted to give you this as a housewarming gift, and also to tell you that I do custom woodwork if you need any cabinets or furniture made for the house."

Misty turned to watch as Craig placed a small but beautiful hand-carved owl on the kitchen counter. "How thoughtful," Misty said, walking over to inspect the owl closer. "This is beautiful, Craig. You're very talented."

"Thank you," he said, blushing a bit. "It's what I love to do."

"Well, I'm glad you came by because I actually would like to have a linen closet built for one of the upstairs bathrooms, and maybe even a couple of rocking chairs and a swing for the front porch," Misty told him as she retrieved two mugs from the cupboard. "Could you give me a quote?"

With a look of pleasure filling his hazel eyes, Craig nodded and said, "I'd love to."

As the two sat down to enjoy their coffee, a thought popped into Misty's head and she immediately jumped at the opportunity.

"So, I heard that your brother dated Cora Griffin for a little while," she stated in a casual tone of voice. "When he was here the other day, he said she dumped him for Hank."

"He was right," Craig nodded with a sigh. "I was away at college when it happened, but I could tell she really hurt him."

"What a shame," Misty said, shaking her head. "She also dated Daniel Abraham, didn't she? Do you know what happened to them?"

Pursing his lips in thought, Craig said, "If I remember correctly, the girl I was dating at the time said she heard Daniel kept getting too rough with Cora and she finally had enough and broke it off. I think her grandfather even got involved and told him to back off."

Eyes wide, Misty leaned closer and asked, "You mean, he hit her or something?"

Looking a bit uncomfortable, Craig shrugged his shoulders and said, "I think so, but I don't know for sure."

"It's hard to imagine that such a nice man could have a violent side," Misty stated, taking a sip of her coffee.

"Yes, it is," Craig agreed.

After he'd gone, Misty tried to do a bit of work around the house but couldn't seem to get her mind off of Daniel Abraham. Finally, she gave in and called Tori, spilling the news as soon as her friend answered.

"Do you want to meet me for lunch at Abraham's Café? We might just happen to see Daniel while we're there, and maybe even have a little chat."

"Do you think that's wise, Misty?" Tori asked, keeping her voice low so her customers wouldn't overhear the conversation. "If he has a violent side, maybe we should leave him alone."

"I'm not going to point blank ask him if he murdered Cora and Hank," Misty told her. "I would just like to feel him out a bit."

Tori finally agreed, and they met at the café at a little past noon. They ordered their food and discussed the case, both stating their own opinions about who the killer could be.

"If you ask me, Rick Harley seems to be the most likely," Tori said, as she took a bite of her cranberry turkey sandwich. "I've never liked him; he always seems so rude."

"Apparently Cora had to have seen something in him, though, to have dated him," Misty pointed out.

"So, maybe he changed when she broke up with him," Tori replied. "He could have been so heartbroken that he snapped."

She had a good point. Sighing, Misty said, "I don't understand why the police aren't taking this more seriously. Two people were murdered, and nothing is being done."

"They think Cora did it," Tori stated with a shrug. "And maybe they're right."

Daniel Abraham stepped out of his office then, and Misty waved to him, trying to catch his eye. When he spotted them, he smiled and headed in their direction.

"I don't think I can do this," Tori muttered, rubbing her head. Standing, she smiled at Daniel and said, "It's good to see you, Mr. Abraham. I, uh, left something in my car, so I'll be right back."

Chicken, Misty thought, pursing her lips as she watched her friend hurry outside.

Blinking in surprise, Daniel turned to Misty and said, "It's good to see you again, Miss Raven. I hope you're settling into your new home well?"

"Please, call me Misty," she said, smiling politely. "I am certainly trying to settle in, but I'm sure you've heard of all the difficulties I've been having."

Nodding his head sympathetically, Daniel said, "Yes, I have, and I'll admit I was shocked to hear about the discovery of Hank's body in your backyard."

"Were the two of you friends?"

"We went to school together," was his short reply.

"And both of you dated Cora," Misty stated, watching him closely.

Daniel jerked back slightly at those words, a tense look passing over his face. Forcing a tight smile, he said, "Yes, but I dated her a couple of years before Hank."

"Why did the two of you break up?" Misty pressed, reaching out to pick up her glass of lemon water.

Daniel hesitated and glanced anxiously around the room, as if hoping that someone would interrupt and give him an excuse to leave. When no one did, he finally cleared his throat and said, "I'm sorry, Miss Raven, but that's personal. Is there anything I can get for you? If not, I really should be getting back to work."

Pushing her luck, Misty leaned forward and said in a low tone, "I heard that you got violent with her, Mr. Abraham. Is that true?"

His cheeks flushing red, Daniel leaned over and hissed, "No, that isn't true, and I would appreciate it if you kept your nosy questions to yourself."

Turning on his heel, Daniel stomped away, leaving Misty with the feeling that what Craig told her was true after all.

Tori returned as soon as Daniel went back into his office, and when Misty told her what happened, her eyes widened and she said, "It sounds like Mr. Abraham really does have a temper after all. I never would have thought it, but maybe that's why he's never married."

They paid the check, and as they walked outside, Misty cocked an eyebrow at Tori and asked, "By the way, did you find what you were looking for in your car?"

With a sheepish laugh, Tori shook her head and said, "Yeah, sorry about that. I've just always thought of Daniel Abraham as being such a nice man that I couldn't bring myself to interrogate him."

"I don't blame you," Misty replied with a shiver. "It turned out to be a most unpleasant experience."

"So, what do we do now?" Tori asked when they reached their cars.

Leaning against her hood, Misty crossed her arms and said, "Now we need to figure out a way

77

to talk to Jeremy Neely. What does he do for a living?"

"He's an author," Tori said, her eyes lighting up as she added excitedly, "And he comes by the coffee shop every Monday morning to write!"

"That's great," Misty clapped her hands. "Is he married?"

Tori shook her head and laughed. "No, his mother would never stand for that."

With a chuckle, Misty thought it over for a moment and said, "Okay, here's the plan: I'll buy one of his books and stop by the coffee shop Monday morning. When I see him, I'll ask him to sign it for me and maybe ask a few questions while I'm at it."

Tori nodded and said pleadingly, "Please don't make him angry, though. I don't want to lose a good customer."

Misty promised to be on her best behavior and then hugged her friend goodbye, stating that she'd see her on Monday.

Misty spent the rest of the day sanding down most of the walls downstairs, eager to get started on the painting. She synced her cellphone to a speaker and played all of her favorite songs, and since there was hardly any furniture, the house echoed with music. She was so engrossed with her work that she hardly noticed how late it was getting, and when she finally glanced at her watch, her eyes widened when she realized it was well past ten o'clock.

Sighing, Misty began gathering up her tools to put everything away. Her music was still playing, but when her cellphone skipped to the next song, Misty thought she heard something in the brief moment of silence. It sounded like it came from the kitchen, and Misty paused the music, listening. When she didn't hear anything, her brow furrowed and she decided to go see for herself.

Maybe it was just the wind, she thought as she walked through the house. *Or a raccoon.*

She pushed the kitchen door open and stopped, blinking in surprise. The lights were off, and she distinctly remembered leaving them on. A chill of foreboding began creeping up her spine as Misty hurriedly reached out for the light switch, her fingers trembling a bit. Suddenly, a dark silhouette moved from behind the door and grabbed her by the hand, jerking her roughly into the kitchen. Misty screamed, the sound reverberating loudly throughout the house, and she desperately began to struggle, her heart racing wildly within her chest. Through the darkness, she could tell the intruder was a man, but he wore a black ski mask over his face and none of his features were discernable.

With a snap of his wrist, he spun Misty around and wrapped his arm around her throat, nearly cutting off her air. Gasping, Misty tried to struggle, her heart pounding fiercely in her chest, but he was too strong for her.

"This is your last warning," he whispered

harshly in her ear, and she stilled. "Leave this place immediately, or you'll be the next one buried in the backyard."

With that being said, he shoved her to the ground and ran out through the back door, his presence sweeping from the room like a vicious, violent tornado.

Pushing herself up on trembling legs, Misty hurried through the house to find her cellphone. She was shaking so badly that she could hardly dial 911, and when the operator answered, her throat was almost too dry to speak.

"S-someone just br-broke into my house," she stuttered. "Please s-send someone out immediately.

CHAPTER 9

The arrival of Officer Lewis and his partner took longer than usual, and Misty was a bundle of nerves by the time they arrived. When they finally knocked on her front door, she quickly ushered them inside and explained what had happened.

"Did you see his face?" Officer Lewis asked while his partner, Officer Mitchell, searched around the perimeter of the house.

"No," Misty shook her head. "He was wearing a ski mask, and the kitchen was dark."

"What about his voice? Did you recognize it?"

Sighing, Misty shook her head once again. "No, he spoke in a whisper."

"I don't see anything outside," Officer Mitchell called out as he came back inside.

Cocking an eyebrow at Misty, Officer Lewis said, "Miss Raven, no offense, but ever since your arrival here, there has been nothing but trouble. May I suggest you lie low and stop asking so many nosy questions? You're stirring up trouble, and I've had just about enough of it."

When Misty's eyes widened, Officer Lewis nodded and said, "Yes, I've heard all about the way you've been prying into other people's business trying to find Cora Griffin's murderer, but you are **not** a detective, Miss Raven, and I'd appreciate it if you'd leave that job to the professionals."

Feeling just a tad annoyed, Misty pursed her lips and said, "I couldn't agree more, except the **professionals** don't seem to be doing anything."

His jaw clenching, Officer Lewis said in a warning tone, "Don't push your luck, Miss Raven, or I'll charge you for interfering with a police investigation. Understood?"

Sighing, Misty nodded and said contritely, "Yes, Officer Lewis, and I apologize for what I said; I'm just upset about what happened, I suppose."

Deflating a bit, Officer Lewis said, "Well…alright. I'll post a man outside tonight to keep an eye on things, but I suggest you either do as the man said and leave town or buy a gun."

With that said, he motioned to his partner and the two began to walk out. Following on their heels, Misty said, "I plan on getting an alarm system installed tomorrow, if possible. Thank you for your help, officer."

Before he left, Officer Lewis turned to look back at Misty and said, "Don't forget what I said; keep your nose out of this investigation."

For the rest of the night, Misty paced around the house, a hammer clutched in her hand. Every few minutes, she'd peer out the front window to make certain the police officer was still sitting out there, his presence only a bit of comfort. What had she gotten herself into? That man could have killed her tonight, and Misty was starting to think she'd gotten too caught up in this investigation. She'd come to Shady Pines for one reason and one reason only, but she'd gotten so involved in trying to solve Cora and Hank's murders that she'd lost her focus.

It's time to get back on track and concentrate on the real reason you're here, she told herself.

At nearly four o'clock a.m., Misty finally sat down in the chair by her bed and drifted off to sleep, the hammer resting lightly in her lap.

The next morning, someone knocked on Misty's front door, and she stumbled through the house to answer it, her eyes bleary and head pounding. When she swung the door open, she was surprised to see Tori standing there…with a dog by her side. And not just any dog, but the biggest one Misty had ever seen.

"Before you say anything, hear me out," Tori blurted, holding up her hands. "I know you said you didn't want a dog right now, but when I heard what happened last night, I decided that you're either going to have a dog or I'm moving in with you. So, which will it be?" Lips pursed, Tori placed her hands on her hips and eyed Misty with a raised eyebrow.

Blinking in surprise, Misty asked, "You've already heard about last night?"

"That's right," Tori nodded. "I open at six, remember? So when Officer Mitchell came in for his morning muffin and coffee, he told me what happened."

"Makes sense," Misty yawned, rubbing her head. "Look, Tori, I plan to get a security system installed as soon as possible, so I don't really think I'll need a dog…"

"What will a security system do to protect you if this maniac decides he wants to kill you?" Tori interrupted, placing a hand on her hip. "Look, I know it's not safe to have a dog inside the house right now with all the renovations going on, but Walnut here can stay on your back porch and keep a lookout. Trust me, the porch will be better than the cage he has to sleep in at the shelter, and if anyone even steps foot on your property, he'll scare them off."

With a sigh, Misty finally gave in. Eyeing the enormous brown and white creature with a bit of uncertainty, she asked, "His name is…Walnut?"

"Wally, for short," Tori grinned, shoving his lead into her hands. "He's a Saint Bernard mix, so he's super sweet and loveable but very protective, so I know he'll be a great watchdog. Won't you, Wally boy?"

Leaning over, Tori rubbed Wally's ears and his fluffy tail began to wag, his huge tongue lolling out the side of his mouth like a giant fruit roll-up.

Misty reached out and gingerly touched the top of his soft head, and when he turned to smell her hand, she held her breath, hoping he wouldn't bite it off. When he stepped closer and bumped against her leg, she sighed with relief; it seemed that her new companion approved of her.

Touched by Tori's concern for her well-being, Misty thanked her new friend and led Wally around to the back porch. He kept his nose to the ground the entire time, stopping every few steps to mark his new territory, and Misty suddenly realized she now had someone other than herself to look after. The thought was a bit frightening, and she hoped she would do a good job.

"I brought along everything he'll need," Tori called out, and Misty turned to see her lugging a massive dog bed, food and water bowl, and a bag of dog food from the back of her car.

"Let me help you with that," Misty said, tying Wally's leash to the porch handrail as she hurried back to help her friend. As they set up a corner for Wally on the back porch, he continued to sniff around and Misty said, "What if he chases after a raccoon or something in the night and gets lost?"

"Just tie his leash to the porch spindles," Tori replied as she filled Wally's bowl up with water. "It's extra long, so he'll still have enough room to move around."

"I hope he'll be okay out here," Misty muttered as she patted Wally on the head. He looked up at her with those big, soulful eyes and licked her hand, and she felt her heart melt.

"So, are you going to give me all the details

about last night or what?" Tori asked, straightening up to plant her hands on her hips.

Misty asked Tori to come inside for some coffee and scones, and while they ate, Misty told her everything.

"I'm starting to think I should take Officer Lewis's advice and mind my own business," Misty said with a sigh. "It seems like I've caused so much trouble since my arrival."

"You're not responsible for all that's happened, Misty," Tori told her. "You've just accidentally stumbled upon a murder that should have been investigated and solved years ago."

"Officer Lewis did say, though, that he'll charge me with interfering in a police investigation if I don't quit asking so many questions," Misty said as she went to the refrigerator to retrieve more coffee creamer.

Blowing a tendril out of her face, Tori reached for another scone and said, "I think he's just upset that you're getting close to the truth and he's not."

Stirring the cream into her coffee, Misty asked, "You really think I'm getting close to the truth?"

"Why else would someone want to keep you quiet so badly?" Tori pointed out. "I understand why you might want to back off, though, because things seem to be getting pretty dangerous."

Leaning back against the kitchen sink, Misty sipped her coffee and thought over everything Tori had just said. Someone did seem to think that Misty was getting too close to the truth, and that someone had to be the person who killed Cora and Hank. Officer Lewis, however, didn't seem to think so; Misty knew he simply believed that someone was trying to scare her off because she was "stirring up so much trouble", so how else would the mystery be solved if she didn't continue trying?

"Yes, things *are* getting a little dangerous," Misty said slowly, "but I *do* have a watchdog now to protect me, and I'll also have the security system."

Her lips twitching, Tori asked, "You're not planning to back off, are you?"

With a bit of fire coming into her gray eyes, Misty placed her hands on her hips and said, "No, I'm not. Two people were murdered in this house, and I refuse to be scared away by some bully who thinks he can break in and push me around."

Shaking her head, Tori said with a laugh, "I figured as much. You don't scare easily, do you?"

"I used to," Misty replied with a small sigh, "but then I realized that I'm the only person I can truly rely on, so I had to learn to stand up for myself."

Twiddling her fingers, Tori said hesitantly, "Brice told me you were raised in the foster system. Did…did you have to move around a lot?"

Nodding, Misty glanced down at her feet for a moment. She didn't enjoy talking about her childhood; the memories were painful, and she rarely discussed the details with anyone. She didn't, however, wish to hurt Tori's feelings by being rude, so she cleared her throat and said, "Yes. I was very sickly as a little girl, and since no one wanted a sick child, I was shuffled around quite a bit. I stayed in my last home for four years, and that was the longest I ever spent with a family."

Her eyes filling with sympathy, Tori asked, "Do you ever see them?"

"Oh, no," Misty shook her head with a short, humorless laugh. "They only wanted me and the other five kids for the money; there was no relationship whatsoever."

For a moment, Misty thought Tori was going to cry, and she shuffled her feet awkwardly, trying to think of a way to change the subject.

"I'm so sorry, Misty," Tori finally said in a soft voice. "You know, I always wanted a sister, and if my parents had only known about you, they could have brought you home to live with us."

Her friend's words warmed Misty's heart, and she had to force herself not to start crying as well. No one had ever been so kind to her before, and only one other girl in middle school had tried to befriend her. Misty was touched by Tori's offer of friendship, and with a smile, she said, "Thanks, Tori. I always wanted a sister, too."

She sat back down at the bar and grabbed another scone, and the conversation shortly drifted back to the case. Before Tori left, she asked, "So, will I be seeing you at the coffee shop Monday morning?"

With a twinkle coming into her eyes, Misty

nodded and said, "You bet."

After Tori was gone, Misty immediately called the alarm system company, only to realize they weren't open on the weekend. With a sigh, she hung up the phone, suddenly very grateful for Wally's presence. Walking outside to see her new friend again, she was immediately greeted by a slobbery kiss.

"I hope you don't make friends this easily with a burglar," Misty stated with a chuckle as she rubbed his ears. When he grabbed a nearby tennis ball that Tori left in his "toy basket", Misty couldn't resist taking him out into the yard to play for a bit. He was very smart and obedient; he brought the ball back every time Misty threw it, and when he got distracted by birds or squirrels, he'd always return to Misty's side when she called to him. It was apparent that whoever had him first had trained him very well, and she wondered how he'd ended up at the shelter. Her heart squeezing with compassion, Misty felt a sudden kinship with this dog. They shared something in common; they'd both been cast aside and placed with strangers, and she decided right then and there to keep him. She knew how it felt not to belong anywhere, and she didn't want Wally to suffer that way any longer.

Once Wally was tired out from playing, he settled down in his bed for a nap and Misty went into town to buy one of Jeremy Neely's books. She hadn't decided what she was going to say to him yet, but she knew she needed to be a bit more careful with her questions. She'd angered Daniel Abraham, and didn't wish to do the same with Jeremy Neely.

When she got back home, Misty spent the rest of the day working in the house, and by the time night arrived, she was exhausted. As she made certain all the doors were locked and the curtains were drawn, she stepped out onto the back porch to check on Wally. When he saw her, he sat up and looked at her, his big eyes so sad that it broke her heart.

"I can't leave you out here like this," she sighed, walking over to untie his leash. "My bedroom doesn't have any exposed nails or tools lying around, so you'll have to promise not to escape into the rest of the house."

As she bent over to pick up his bed, Wally let out a low growl and the hair on the back of Misty's neck stood up. Jumping back, she looked down at him to find that he was facing the backyard, his tail down and ears flat against his head. Spinning around, Misty peered into the yard to see a dark shadow walking slowly toward them.

"You're not gone yet?"

Holding Wally's lead tightly in her hands, Misty let out a slight breath of relief as she said, "Mr. Thomas, you scared me nearly half to death. What are you doing out here so late at night?"

Slowly stepping up onto her porch, Mr. Thomas's face came into view and Misty shrank back at the look of disdain in his brown eyes.

"Don't you know Cora wants to be left alone here?" he hissed, and Wally growled again.

Squaring her shoulders, Misty said in a firm tone, "Mr. Thomas, Cora is dead. I am the new owner of this place, and I'm sorry that you don't want me here but I'm *not* leaving anytime soon, so please stop trying to frighten me."

"It's for your own good," he said, taking a step closer, and Misty thought she saw a look of urgency in his gaze. "If you stay, you're liable to end up like them."

Her brow furrowing, Misty asked slowly, "Mr. Thomas, do you know something about Cora and Hank's deaths?"

Mr. Thomas didn't answer; he simply stood there staring, almost as if he'd gone off into a trance. Finally, he shook his head and turned to walk away, his shadow fading back into the darkness until he could no longer be seen.

With a sigh, Misty gathered up Wally's things, led him inside, and bolted the kitchen door. As she settled into bed a bit later, the door to her own bedroom also locked, she watched as Wally slept peacefully by her bed, and she was once again very grateful for the thoughtfulness of her friend. She felt safer with Wally by her side and decided that maybe it wasn't best to be alone after all.

CHAPTER 10

The next afternoon, Misty was pleasantly surprised to receive a call from Adam. She hadn't heard from him since their "date" last weekend and had started to wonder if perhaps he hadn't enjoyed himself.

"I stayed over in Savannah for the weekend," he told her, "and wondered if you'd like to drive down and meet me for an early supper?"

A bit surprised by the invitation, Misty hesitated. "Oh, I don't know…" she said.

"Come on, I thought you said you loved Savannah?" he persisted, and finally, with a small laugh, she gave in.

Adam was right; Misty was always happy to have any excuse to go to Savannah, and after hurriedly getting ready, she met Adam at a little past four at The Shrimp Factory, one of her favorite restaurants on River Street. Once a cotton warehouse built in 1823, the old building overlooked the Savannah River and was one of the city's best places to eat seafood.

After ordering a plate of shrimp and grits, Misty sat back in her chair and sighed, happy to relax and enjoy herself for a while. It had been quite a long and eventful weekend, and she hoped things would begin to settle down a bit.

"So, tell me," Adam said after the server left their drinks, "how and why did you start renovating homes?"

Misty leaned back in her chair and smiled as the memories filled her mind. "There was an elderly gentleman who lived next door to my last foster family," she explained, lightly picking at the cuff of her crimson sweater. "His wife was dead and his children had all moved away, so he was just as lonely as I was. He became like a grandfather to me; I would spend as much time with him as I possibly could, and since he was a retired contractor, he taught me everything he knew. He would still get calls to do smaller jobs from time to time, and he often took me with him." Chuckling softly, Misty shook her head and added, "I remember saying once that girls rarely work in the construction realm, but he told me I shouldn't let that hold me back because I had a special gift of turning old castaways into something new and beautiful. He said if you find something you're good at, don't worry about what anyone else says."

"He sounds like a very wise man," Adam said with a kind smile.

"He was," Misty nodded, the light in her eyes fading with sadness. "He died when I was eighteen, and I remember feeling such an overwhelming sense of grief. He really meant the world to me and was the only real family I've ever known. He left his house to me and told me to fix it up and sell it. I kept it for a couple of years, but something…" she hesitated, clearing her throat, "well, something came up, and I needed money, so I had to sell it. I hated to let go of that place, but maybe someday I'll return and try to buy it back."

"I'd prefer that you stay in Shady Pines," Adam stated in a warm tone, and Misty glanced away, her cheeks flushing.

The server brought their food then, and Misty was grateful for the interruption. Whatever his interest in her, Misty wasn't ready for anything other than friendship, and Adam seemed to sense this because he changed the subject and began talking about all the excitement going on in town.

"Mom called and told me someone broke into your house and threatened you," he said as he cut into his thick, juicy steak. "It seems your arrival in town has stirred things up."

"That certainly wasn't my intention," Misty replied, laughing sheepishly. "It just seems like trouble has a way of finding me. I only hope that whoever killed Hank and Cora will be caught and put behind bars."

After supper, they walked along River Street, and Misty bought a bag of homemade dog treats for Wally as well as a box of pecan pralines for herself. It turned out to be quite an enjoyable evening, and when Adam walked Misty back to her car, she thanked him for the invite.

"Will I see you at the harvest party this coming weekend?" he wanted to know.

"With my knack for getting into trouble, maybe

I should stay home," Misty replied with a laugh.

"We'll just have to make sure you stay out of trouble," Adam said warmly. "Please say you'll come; it's a lot of fun, and I'm sure you'll enjoy it. Plus, everyone in town shows up, so you can't stay home."

Misty raised her eyebrows. "Everyone?"

"That's right," he nodded.

"Well then, I guess I shouldn't miss something so important," she replied, thinking that the party could be a golden opportunity to meet many people and ask a lot of questions.

"Good," Adam stated, his black eyes sparkling. "I'll see you there then."

The next morning, Misty stepped into Tori's coffee shop with Jeremy Neely's book in hand, her eyes skimming across the room until she spotted him sitting in the far right-hand corner with a cup of coffee and a laptop computer. Casually walking up to the counter, Misty winked at Tori as she ordered an apple fritter and pumpkin spice latte.

"He's been here for nearly an hour," Tori said in a low voice, "so you'd better make your move before he leaves."

Nodding, Misty grabbed her food and headed in the direction of his table. She hoped he would be friendlier than his mother and quickly rehearsed the speech she'd prepared in her head.

"Mr. Neely?" she asked, stopping at his table. When he looked up at her questioningly, she held out the book and said with a smile, "I'm sorry to bother you, but would you mind signing this for me? I just bought it and can't wait to read it."

His eyes lighting up, Jeremy Neely shut his laptop and motioned to the chair opposite him. "Of course not. Why don't you have a seat while I find a pen?"

Pleasantly surprised at the kind invitation, Misty sat down and handed him the book. He dug around his laptop case until he found a pen and then signed the book with quick movements and exaggerated flourish.

"There you go. I hope you enjoy reading it," he stated with a wide smile as he returned the book. Leaning back in his chair, he eyed her for a moment and asked, "You're the girl that just bought the old bed-and-breakfast, aren't you?"

How did everyone seem to know who she was? Nodding, Misty sighed heavily and said, "Yes, I'm the unlucky girl that's tripped into a hornet's nest and can't seem to find my way out."

"You poor thing," he *tsked* sympathetically. "How awful it must have been to have found Hank's body buried in your backyard."

Shivering, Misty nodded and said, "It certainly was, and now it seems someone wants me to leave for good."

Leaning toward her, Jeremy lowered his voice and asked, "What do you mean?"

"Haven't you heard?"

"No, I've been so wrapped up in my latest book that apparently I've missed something important," he replied, his eyes alight with curiosity.

Taking a bite of her apple fritter, Misty told him about the man breaking into her home and threatening her. With a gasp, Jeremy rested his hand on his chest and exclaimed, "How terrifying! Do the police know who's responsible?"

Pursing her lips, Misty said, "No, and I don't expect them to. I'm honestly starting to wonder if Officer Lewis thinks I'm making this stuff up."

"I never did like that man," he muttered, sitting back in his chair with a huff.

"Mr. Neely, I know this is a bit random, but would you mind if I asked what happened between you and Cora?"

Jeremy glanced at her in surprise, and Misty awaited his reaction with bated breath.

"Certainly not," Jeremy replied with a wave of his hand. "We were only twenty or twenty-one, and neither of us was the settling down types. We dated for a little while, had some good times together, and then just decided to move on. We both got bored, I suppose."

"I see," Misty replied as she sipped the delicious latte. "Cora was going to settle down with Hank, though, wasn't she?"

Jeremy made a *pffft* sound with his mouth and said, "I doubt it; they'd actually broken up when Cora died. Cora didn't want to be tied down, and I know that for a fact because...," he hesitated, clearing his throat awkwardly as he shrugged and said, "Well, because she told me so."

Raising her eyebrows, Misty asked, "She told you that before she died?"

Shifting in his seat uncomfortably, Jeremy nodded and said, "Yes, as a matter of fact, she did."

How strange, Misty thought. If Cora really told Jeremy that before she died, then why had she seemed so eager to talk things out with Hank when he sent her the flowers? Had Misty misread the situation somehow?

Shaking the thoughts from her mind, Misty looked at Jeremy and asked, "Mr. Neely, you wouldn't happen to know who Cora's other beau was, do you? I know she dated you, Daniel Abraham, and Rick Harley, but I heard there was someone else. Do you know who it was?"

When Jeremy nodded and said, "I certainly do," Misty felt her heart kick into overdrive. Leaning anxiously toward him, she asked, "Who was it?"

With a slight smile, he said, "Officer Harlem Lewis."

As Misty drove home, she played the conversation with Jeremy Neely over and over in her mind. Officer Lewis was Cora's mysterious ex? Misty couldn't believe it, and she was starting

98

to wonder if this was the reason he was so determined to blame Cora for Hank's death. Was he possibly trying to defer the suspicion away from himself? The note Misty found in Cora's closet had simply been signed "-H"; what if it was actually from Harlem, instead of Hank?

After she got home, Misty called the alarm company and requested to have a system installed as soon as possible.

"I'm sorry, honey," the woman said, "but it's fall break, and our installer took his kids to Disney for the week."

"You only have one installer?" Misty asked, raising her eyebrows.

"Yes, ma'am, but he'll be back next week."

With a sigh, Misty left her information and hung up, feeling more grateful for Wally than ever. Thinking that she should perhaps get something a little extra for protection, she ordered two Taser guns; one for her car and the other to keep in the drawer by her bed.

Her phone rang just then, and Misty immediately answered when she saw who it was.

"He's gone," Tori blurted before Misty could even utter a full "hello". "So? What did he say?"

When Misty told her everything Jeremy said, Tori gasped in surprise. "How did I not know about this? And how awful that he's the main one who believes she killed herself!"

Misty told Tori about the card she'd found in Cora's closet and said, "What if *he's* the one who sent it? What if he came over to see her the night she died and they got into an argument or something?"

"This is crazy," Tori sighed, and Misty could imagine her friend shaking her head.

Just then, Misty could hear the bell above the door jingle, and Tori said, "A customer just walked in, so I've got to go. Hey, you're coming to the harvest party this Saturday, right?"

Misty nodded. "Yes, I'm planning on it."

"Good," Tori replied. "Why don't you bring Wally with you? The kids will love him, and it seems that people are more friendly and apt to…well…talk and answer questions when a dog is around, if you know what I mean."

"That's not a bad idea," Misty stated as she walked into the kitchen to check on her new furry beast of a pet. "I think I'll do that. See you there."

CHAPTER 11

efore she knew it, Saturday arrived and it was time for the harvest party. Misty wore a new rust brown dress with a pair of cowgirl boots, and pulled her hair back into a loose, low ponytail with a few tendrils left hanging around her face. She'd never been to a harvest party before, and as she opened the back door to her car for Wally to hop inside, she found herself feeling very excited.

The park was filled with people when Misty arrived, and after hooking Wally to his leash, she went in search of Tori and finally found her running the booth for the animal shelter.

"I don't know how you have time to run your own business *and* volunteer at the local pet shelter," Misty stated, smiling at her friend.

"Oh, who needs downtime anyway?" Tori waved a hand and laughed. Surveying Misty's outfit, she said, "You look adorable! I love the boots."

Kids immediately began surrounding Wally, and Misty let some of the older ones take him for a walk; he always did so great on the leash that she knew she had no reason to worry.

Turning to survey the park, Misty took note of

the other booths dotting the lengthy landscape, as well as the small petting zoo, moon bounce, and stage set up for music and dancing later. She could smell the amazing aroma of barbeque, baked beans, and turkey legs, and felt her stomach rumble.

"Hello, ladies," a voice spoke from behind, and Misty turned to find Craig Harley standing there, smiling.

"Hello, Craig," Misty said with a small, friendly wave.

"Hi," Tori greeted him. "Are you having a good time?"

"So far, so good," he replied with a nod. Motioning to the stage, he said to Tori, "I hope you'll save me a dance later."

Tori blinked, her face blushing red, and Misty had to hide her smile.

"Oh, y-yes, I sure will," she replied, clearing her throat awkwardly.

Nodding to them both, Craig walked away and Misty said with a mischievous gleam in her eye, "Maybe you should save him *two* dances."

"Oh, stop," Tori laughed. "I already told you; we're just friends."

Misty spent the next hour helping Tori run the shelter booth and was pleased to have the opportunity to meet so many people. It seemed that everyone in town stopped by to speak to Tori and pet the dogs, and Tori made a point of introducing Misty to them all.

"Misty, this is Mr. Patrick Donovan," Tori said when one gentleman in his mid-fifties stopped by the booth. "He worked in education for over thirty years until he recently retired; he was actually my science teacher in fifth grade."

"It's very nice to meet you, Mr. Donovan," Misty said as she shook the man's hand.

"Welcome to Shady Pines, Miss Raven," he said, smiling pleasantly. "I hope you'll love our small town as much as I do."

The time passed quickly, and Misty found she was having a blast. The dogs were so sweet and eager for attention, and everyone that stopped by was very nice and friendly. Five dogs got adopted, and Misty couldn't help but rub Wally's head a few extra times in gratitude for his presence in her life. If not for Tori, he would quite possibly still be stuck in a cage wishing for love and freedom, and Misty was so happy her friend took it upon herself to put them together. When Misty told Tori she'd decided to adopt him, her friend clapped her hands and squealed with delight.

"What's all the commotion about?" a familiar voice asked from behind, and Misty turned to smile at Brice.

"I've decided to adopt Wally," she told him, while Tori helped a customer.

"That's wonderful news," he replied, his deep blue eyes twinkling. "It's about time you let someone into your life."

Wally barked and bumped against Brice's legs,

hoping to get a back rub, and nearly threw him off balance. With a chuckle, Brice reached down to tussle with him.

"Why don't you two go have some fun?" Tori asked. "We're closing the booth in about an hour, and then I'll join you. Misty, you can leave Wally here with me if you like."

"Come on," Brice said, taking Misty's hand and giving it a playful tug when she hesitated. "You've got to try our local cotton candy."

Following him, Misty's brow furrowed as she said, "You make it sound different from regular cotton candy."

"Oh, it is," he replied with a snicker, and Misty couldn't help but notice the flirtatious looks he received as they made their way through the crowd. Brice was quite a handsome man; the blue plaid shirt he wore brought out the color of his eyes and the broadness of his shoulders. His sandy blonde hair was shiny and thick, and Misty suddenly found herself wondering how soft it must feel.

Shaking herself, Misty forced such thoughts right out of her mind as they stopped in front of the cotton candy stand.

"*Pickle* flavored cotton candy?" she asked incredulously.

Laughing at the look of disgust on her face, Brice said, "The bacon one is my favorite."

"That's disgusting," Misty stated with a slight shiver.

"Don't knock it 'til you've tried it," he replied, handing his money to the man at the booth.

"I think I'll try the cinnamon bun flavor," Misty told the man.

As they walked along, both enjoying their cotton candy, Misty spotted Daniel Abraham and excused herself for a moment. She didn't wish to get a bad name around town for badgering people with rude, nosy questions, so she'd decided to apologize the next time she saw him.

"Excuse me, Mr. Abraham," she said as she drew closer to him. When he saw her, Misty thought for a split second that he would turn and bolt in the opposite direction, and she quickly said, "I'd like to apologize for the other day, Mr. Abraham. I was much too pushy, and I'm very sorry if I offended you."

Hesitating, Daniel glanced around as if to make certain no one was listening, and in a low tone of voice, he said, "It...it's quite alright. I was just upset that such a terrible rumor was going around about me."

"Well, I'm sure it couldn't be true of a nice, upstanding man such as yourself, and I'm sorry," she said with a smile, studying him closely. In her opinion, his brown eyes looked a bit clouded with worry, and he reached up to run his hand nervously over his thinning brown hair.

"No, of course it's not true," he replied. Clearing his throat, he backed away and said, "Well, it was good to see you, Miss Raven. I hope you enjoy yourself."

"What was that about?" Brice asked when she returned.

"Just a little damage control," she replied, smiling mysteriously when he raised his eyebrows.

As the sun began to set, Tori joined Misty and Brice with Wally in tow, and they all chatted amiably as they strolled slowly through the booths. Misty bought some handmade soap, a jar of peach preserves, and a hand-knitted scarf, fully immersing herself in the excitement of the evening. She also ate two turkey legs, a bowl of Brunswick Stew, and a piece of homemade fudge.

"You're not going to feel like dancing if you keep eating," Brice teased her.

"Who says I want to dance?" Misty asked as she wiped her hands on a napkin and then threw it away.

"Why would you *not* want to dance with a charming fella such as myself?" he asked, wiggling his eyebrows.

Misty couldn't help but laugh, and Tori rolled her eyes and said, "You keep that up and you'll run her off."

The music started up then, and Misty saw Craig heading their way. Elbowing Tori, Misty nodded in his direction and chuckled when her friend started blushing once again.

"Have fun," Misty winked at her as she walked off with Craig. Turning to glance up at Brice, Misty was surprised to see that he was frowning.

"What's that look for?"

"I don't like where that's going," he stated, nodding at the retreating couple.

"Why not?" Misty tilted her head curiously. "Don't you like Craig?"

"Honestly?" Brice asked, looking down at Misty. "No, not really."

Misty blinked in surprise. "Why not?"

Sighing, Brice rubbed the back of his neck and said, "For one thing, he's too old for her."

"Is that all?" Misty laughed, shaking her head. "There are far worse things than that. Besides, everyone knows a woman is far more mature than a man."

Raising his eyebrows, Brice looked at her and asked, "Is that so? You keep talking like that, and I won't force you to dance with me."

Misty shook her head, and with a grin, Brice tied Wally's leash to a nearby post, took Misty's hand, and led her out onto the dance floor. The music was slow and smooth, and Misty let Brice pull her close, the smell of his woodsy aftershave tickling her senses.

"So, Misty Raven," he said after a moment, his breath soft against her cheek, "with eyes the color of gray mist and hair as black as a raven, how did you get a name that suits you so perfectly?"

"It's not my real name."

Pulling back to look at her in surprise, Brice asked, "It's not?"

"No," Misty shook her head. "It was given to me

when I became a ward of the state."

"How old were you?"

"Three," she replied, absently smoothing down a wrinkle on his shoulder. "I wouldn't talk, though, when I was taken to the police station in Atlanta, so I wasn't able to tell them my real name."

"Who took you to the police station?" Brice questioned.

"I don't know," Misty said softly. She didn't like talking about her past and wished the subject hadn't been broached. "My records were lost in a fire when I was seven, and the only thing anyone remembers is that I was brought in by a man of the cloth and he said I was abandoned at his church. No one remembers what church, or even if it was in Atlanta."

"Do…do *you* remember anything?" Brice asked hesitantly, as if sensing the subject was a sensitive one.

Misty glanced away and shook her head. "My memories are a blur, like a camera when it's out of focus," she said, the scene over his shoulder filled with laughing, happy couples. "I have dreams sometimes, but they're vague and foggy, and I'm not sure how much of it is real and how much is just my imagination. When I was young, the doctors said that what happened must have been very traumatic and I most likely blocked it all out."

The song ended then, and Brice took a step back, still holding her hand as he said gently, "I'm so sorry, Misty. Maybe someday you'll remember."

Smiling, Misty nodded, but before she could reply, she spotted Adam out of the corner of her eye. He was wearing a hunter green pullover sweater, a pair of dark jeans, and brown Timberland sneaker boots. He looked very handsome, and he was heading their way with a smile on his face.

"Hello, you two," he greeted them, clapping Brice on the shoulder. Looking at Misty, he said warmly, "You look beautiful. May I have this next dance?"

Brice stepped away, a slight frown on his face as Adam pulled Misty into his arms.

"Are you having a good time?" Adam asked, his black eyes sparkling in the moonlight.

"Yes, very much so," Misty replied with a nod. "This is my first harvest party; actually, tonight is the first time I've danced since high school."

Raising his eyebrows in surprise, Adam said, "You mean to tell me that men haven't been fighting to take you out dancing?"

Laughing, Misty shrugged and said, "I haven't really had much time for boyfriends."

"So, you've never been married?"

A bit caught off guard by the question, Misty shook her head and said, "No, I haven't. Have you?"

"No, I've been waiting for the right girl to show up," he replied, his gaze warm.

Just then, two familiar faces caught Misty's eye, and she glanced over Adam's shoulder to see

Daniel Abraham and Rick Harley standing among the shadows, having what appeared to be a pretty heated discussion. Daniel was waving his hands, and Rick's face was quickly turning the shade of a tomato. Even though she couldn't see much in the dark setting, Misty thought she caught the words "Cora" and "you owe me" coming from Daniel's mouth as she tried to read his lips.

"Is something interesting happening back there?" Adam asked with a chuckle as he glanced over his shoulder.

"It seems that Mr. Abraham and Mr. Harley are having some sort of argument," Misty replied, watching as Daniel pulled what appeared to be a piece of paper from his pocket and waved it in front of Rick's nose.

"Hmm, it's unusual for Mr. Abraham to be so upset," Adam stated as he, too, watched the two men.

Finally, Rick's wife came onto the scene, and with a firm grip on her husband's arm, she spat something off at Daniel and then pulled Rick away. They walked toward the parking lot, and Misty assumed they must be leaving.

"I wonder what that was all about," she muttered just as the song ended.

"Who knows?" Adam shook his head as they stepped from the dance floor. "It seems like everyone is on edge these days."

Misty and Adam joined Brice, Tori, and Craig then, and Misty said to Craig, "Your brother and

Mr. Abraham seemed to be having an argument just now."

With a look of surprise, Craig said, "Really? I wonder what it was about. Where is my brother?"

"He and his wife just left," Adam stated.

"I'll have to ask him about it when I see him tomorrow," Craig said, shrugging. "Who knows if he'll even tell me, though. My brother can be somewhat…difficult at times."

As they walked toward the pumpkin carving contest, Misty couldn't help but wonder about the argument, and when she glanced around in search of Daniel Abraham, it seemed that he was gone, as well.

CHAPTER 12

By nine o'clock, the festival had died down, and Misty was sad to see the wonderful evening come to an end. Tori had to stay and clean up the shelter booth, and Misty and Brice stayed to help. By the time everything was cleaned up and the remaining dogs were taken back to the shelter, it was after ten o'clock and the park was empty.

Saying her goodbyes, Misty loaded Wally up into her car and headed home. She'd thought that he would be exhausted after such an eventful day, but with bright eyes, he sat up in the back seat with his enormous head hanging happily from the open window and his tail bumping the console as it wagged back and forth.

The night was dark, and when Misty turned down her road, she noticed that a truck turned in behind her. Glancing in her rearview mirror, Misty tried to see who it was, but the headlights were too bright and she immediately began to feel concerned. Who would be coming to her house at such a late hour? It had to be the same man that threatened her before, and with trembling fingers, Misty reached into the glove department and pulled out the Taser gun.

Pulling up in front of her house, Misty parked

and got out, clutching the weapon in her hand as the truck's headlights swept over her. Should she grab Wally and run inside? Even if she was able to get into her house, a simple lock on the door wouldn't keep a man out, and Misty had the sudden thought that she should call the police. Quickly reaching into her purse, her stomach sank when she realized she'd left her phone in the house.

Wally barked, and Misty opened the back door, clutching his leash as he bounded out. Perhaps whoever it was would think twice when he saw the massive dog, as well as the Taser gun she held in her hand. Her heart pounding, she stood there and waited, her body trembling as fear and adrenaline rushed through her veins.

The truck parked, and Misty saw the driver's door swing open. A shadow began moving toward her, but Misty stood her ground, ready to fight for her life at any given moment.

"Where is your phone?" a familiar voice called out. "I've been calling it ever since we left the park."

"Brice, for Pete's sake," Misty breathed as she sank back against her car in relief. "You scared me half to death. My phone is inside; I forgot to take it with me."

"I'm sorry I scared you," he said as he came to stand before her. Reaching down to rub Wally behind the ears, he explained, "I wanted to ask if you'd like to come with me for a late night ride;

there's something I want to show you."

Looking at him quizzically, Misty asked, "What do you want to show me?"

Grinning mysteriously, he said, "It's a surprise. Come on, it'll be fun; you can even bring old Wally here with you."

With a sigh, Misty finally gave in and climbed into Brice's truck. He put Wally into the truck bed, making certain to fasten his leash to the toolbox so he couldn't jump out, and they headed off.

After driving several miles, Brice turned down a small dirt road, and they bumped slowly along for another mile or so until they came to a bend in the road. Misty could see the glow of lights just ahead, and when they rounded the corner, she gasped with delight. A farmhouse rested several yards away from the road, and the entire front yard was decorated for fall. Orange and gold lights twinkled from the trees and bushes, glowing jack-o'-lanterns sat atop large bales of hay, and scarecrows danced along the yard beneath golden archways. It was absolutely breathtaking, and Misty sat gazing at it in silence for a moment, unable to tear her eyes away.

"Well?" Brice asked after a moment, a smile in his voice. "What do you think?"

"It's beautiful; I've never seen anything like it," Misty breathed, rolling the window down to lean her head out.

"They do the same thing for Christmas, so we'll have to come back then."

Turning to smile at him, Misty said, "Thank you for bringing me here, Brice. This was a wonderful surprise."

As they drove back to Misty's house, they talked about the harvest party and the fun they had, and then discussed how the renovations were going on Misty's house. Before she knew it, they were pulling back into Misty's driveway, and she thanked Brice again for the kind surprise.

Misty reached out to grasp the door handle but stopped, a frown pulling at her face as she stared at her house.

"What's wrong?" Brice asked.

"I...I'm almost positive I left the foyer light on when I left this afternoon, but it looks like it's off," Misty replied, her voice a bit worried.

Unbuckling his seatbelt, Brice said, "I'll come in with you and check things out."

Retrieving Wally from the back of the truck, Misty followed Brice onto the porch and unlocked the front door. The house was dark and quiet when she opened the door, and when Wally's tail lowered and he uttered a low growl, Misty felt the hair on her arms stand on end.

"Something isn't right," Brice said, and Misty could hear the concern in his voice.

Feeling along the wall, Misty flipped on the light switch, and the foyer was immediately bathed in a soft glow while the rest of the house remained covered in darkness. Suddenly, a low moan sounded in the direction of Misty's bedroom, and a chill swept up her spine as Wally growled once again.

Picking up a nearby hammer, Brice said, "stay here," and crept slowly toward the closed door. Misty waited with bated breath, ready to release Wally to go help Brice if he needed it. The dog strained against the leash, his teeth bared as he continued to growl, and Misty thought that her heart would pound right out of her chest.

"Misty," Brice finally called, alarm in his voice. "Come here."

Hurrying into her bedroom, Misty gasped at the sight before her. There, near the closet, lay a moaning Mr. Thomas in a puddle of blood. Brice had his cellphone out as he quickly dialed 911, and Misty hurried to her neighbor's side.

"Mr. Thomas, what happened?" she asked, tears coming to her eyes when she saw the oozing gash on the back of his head.

"H-he thought I...was you," Mr. Thomas whispered, his breathing labored.

"Who did?" Misty asked as she pressed a towel against the wound.

Mr. Thomas's lips moved in response, but no sound came out, and Misty watched in horror as his eyes drifted closed and a small, single breath was the last to be released from his frail, broken body.

By the time the police arrived, Misty was beside herself. Mr. Thomas was lying dead on her bedroom floor, and his last words were to warn Misty that the intruder had intended to kill *her* instead of him. To say that she was shaken to the core was an understatement. Mr. Thomas was dead because of her, and as Brice wrapped a supportive arm around her shoulders and led her into the living room, she was grateful for his comforting presence.

It seemed to take hours for Officer Lewis and his team to investigate the area, and when they finally wheeled Mr. Thomas's body from the house, Misty felt drained; both physically and mentally.

"Miss Raven, I don't know what to say at this point," Officer Lewis said, his jaw clenching. "You have come to town and caused more trouble than we've had around here in fifteen years, and now a man is dead because of it."

"This isn't Misty's fault, Officer Lewis," Brice spoke up in Misty's defense. "She can't be blamed for the fact that a body was buried in her backyard, or for everything that's happened since. There's a murderer on the loose, and *you* need to find him."

"I intend to do just that," Officer Lewis snapped, his face flushing, "if I can keep from running out here every other day."

Taking a deep breath, he turned to look at Misty and said, "It seems that the killer thought you were home since your car was parked out front, and he must have been scared off when you and Brice pulled up or I'm sure he would have finished Mr. Thomas off immediately."

Wiping her eyes, Misty asked, "W-why do you think Mr. Thomas was in my house in the first place?"

"I don't have the slightest idea," Officer Lewis said, shrugging. "Loren was an odd bird, so who knows what he was up to."

"Are you going to look for fingerprints or anything?" Brice asked, taking Misty's hand protectively.

Pursing his lips in irritation, Officer Lewis said, "Yes, of course we are. Miss Raven, is there somewhere else you can stay tonight and tomorrow while we give the house a thorough search?"

"She can stay with Tori," Brice stated. When Misty began to protest, he held up his hand and said, "She wouldn't have it any other way, trust me. Now go pack your things and we'll get going."

After throwing a few things into an overnight bag, Misty loaded Wally into her car and followed Brice to Tori's house. As she drove, Misty called Tori to give her a heads up, and when she told her everything that happened, Tori gasped in horror.

"Misty, are you alright?" she immediately asked, her voice filled with worry.

"I'm fine; I just can't believe this is happening," Misty replied with a heavy sigh. "Are you sure I won't be imposing if I stay with you tonight?"

"Of course not," she insisted. "You can stay with

me for as long as you like."

Tori's house was in a small neighborhood just outside of town, and when they arrived and Misty climbed from her car, she felt bone weary. Grabbing Wally's leash, she walked inside and was immediately ushered to the guest bedroom.

"I changed the sheets and left fresh towels in the guest bathroom," Tori told her. She'd apparently been awakened by Misty's phone call, for she was wearing a baggy pair of pajamas and her hair was a mess. Misty felt terrible for dragging her out of bed and putting her to all the extra work of having a guest, and with a sigh, she sank down onto the bed and thanked Tori for everything.

"I can leave Wally outside or put him in the laundry room," she told Tori when Wally nudged her knee with his nose.

"He can stay in here with you; it doesn't matter to me either way," Tori said as she leaned over to rub Wally's back.

Brice carried Misty's overnight bag into the room and told the girls goodnight. "Thank you, Brice, for everything," Misty told him with a tired smile.

"Call me if you need anything," he said before he left.

That night, Misty lay in bed and listened to Wally's soft snores as he slept peacefully by her side, a tear slipping silently down her cheek. She was growing attached to this place, something she'd never allowed to happen before, and the thought of someone dying because of her was making her rethink her decision to come here in the first place.

Maybe she should just leave before anyone else got hurt.

CHAPTER 13

Misty had another dream that night, and when she awoke the next morning, she climbed out of bed with renewed vigor. She might not be able to solve the mystery of her recurring dreams, but someone had tried to kill her last night, and she was determined to find who it was.

Tori had already left for work when Misty stepped into the kitchen, but she'd left a note on the counter telling Misty to help herself to anything she wanted in the refrigerator or pantry. After feeding Wally and fixing herself a bowl of cereal and a cup of coffee, Misty got dressed and drove into town. She had a plan of where she wanted to start, and she hurried into Tori's coffee shop to ask for help.

"Good morning," Tori greeted her when she walked inside. "Did you sleep well?"

Nodding, Misty got right to the point. "I want to search Daniel Abraham's office, and I need your help."

Her eyes wide, Tori asked, "Why do you want to search his office?"

Misty quickly told Tori about the argument between Daniel and Rick, and what she thought she "heard" them say.

"I want to see if I can find whatever it was Daniel was waving in front of Rick's face," she explained.

"Why do you think it'll be in his office?" Tori asked, her brow furrowing.

Misty shrugged. "I just thought that was a good place to start." Her eyes lighting up, she grabbed Tori's arm and asked, "Wait, does Mr. Abraham live in the apartment over the restaurant?"

Sighing, Tori nodded and said, "Yes, but please don't tell me you plan to break into his apartment."

Misty chewed on her bottom lip for a moment. Finally, she smiled slyly and said, "Let's try his office first; I think I've got a plan."

Misty stepped into the restaurant bathroom, keeping the door cracked so she could see the table where Tori sat fidgeting nervously. She'd requested to speak to Mr. Abraham, and when Misty saw him leave his office and walk toward Tori, she hurried from the bathroom and made her way to his office door, hoping no one would notice her.

The door was unlocked, and Misty slipped quietly inside and shut it behind her. The room was dark as she carefully made her way over to the desk, where she quickly flipped the lamp on. Daniel's desk was very neat and tidy, with a laptop computer resting in the middle, an old calculator to the right, and a notepad to the left. Telling herself to hurry, Misty opened the drawers and began carefully going through them.

The clock by Daniel's desk ticked loudly in the quiet room, and Misty felt herself growing more and more nervous; he would be back any moment, and she hadn't found one thing yet. Just when she was about to give up, she noticed a metal box tucked carefully away at the back of the center drawer, and she quickly pulled it out to investigate. The box was locked, and Misty began to feel around under the desk, hoping to find the key. When her fingers landed on the small, cool piece of metal dangling from a nail, she sighed with relief and quickly unlocked the box. When she opened the lid, she found several sheets of paper folded up inside.

It turned out to be copies of old bank statements, and on each page was a highlighted deposit into Daniel's bank account from Rick Harley. The first deposit was from fourteen years ago, and it seemed that Rick had given Daniel fifteen thousand dollars every year since.

Just then, Misty heard the sound of approaching footsteps, and she quickly shoved the papers back into the box and replaced it in the center drawer. The doorknob to the office jiggled, and Misty felt her heart kick into overdrive as she switched off the lamp and dove underneath the desk. The office door opened, and a bit of light from the hallway made its way across the floor as Misty heard

Daniel fumble along the wall for the light switch. If he was coming to sit at his desk, Misty knew she would be discovered and, most likely, arrested.

Unless he simply killed her like he quite possibly did Cora and Hank. But if that were so, why was he apparently blackmailing Rick Harley? Did Rick kill them, and Daniel found out about it?

Before the office light switched on, Misty heard one of the servers call out to Daniel, and she sighed with relief when he turned and left the room, shutting the door behind him. Whether he'd killed them or not, a blackmailer wasn't someone she wanted to tangle with, and Misty got out of there as fast as her trembling legs could carry her.

"Well?" Tori whispered when Misty arrived back at the table, out of breath. "Please tell me you found something; I thought I was going to die when Mr. Abraham excused himself and headed for his office."

"So did I," Misty replied with a sigh. Lowering her voice, Misty leaned across the table and told Tori what she'd found.

Her eyes wide, Tori asked, "But why on earth would Daniel be blackmailing Rick? And why would Rick allow it?"

"Daniel must have something pretty big on Rick," Misty replied. Raising an eyebrow, she added, "Such as...murder?"

Tori's mouth dropped open. "But why wouldn't Daniel just go to the police and tell them what he knows?"

Misty shrugged. "If he did that, he wouldn't have made an extra fifteen thousand dollars a year."

"I can't understand why Rick would go along with that, though," Tori replied, shaking her head. "If he's a murderer, why doesn't he just get rid of Daniel, too?"

"Fifteen thousand dollars isn't *that* much money to someone who makes a good living," Misty replied. "Especially if it'll keep Daniel quiet. And who knows, maybe Daniel has some sort of evidence hidden somewhere that would be found by the police if Rick killed him."

"This just blows my mind," Tori sighed as she rubbed her head. "Who knew our little town had so many secrets?"

Cocking an eyebrow, Misty said, "I imagine there are many more that have yet to be discovered."

That afternoon, Officer Lewis called Misty to tell her she could go back home whenever she wished.

"It looks like whoever killed Loren was wearing gloves, because we didn't find any fingerprints," he told her. "Also, I forgot to ask you last night, but could you bring that note you found by the station? I'd like to keep it for…evidence."

Misty suspected he wanted it for more than evidence, but she agreed to drop it off as soon as possible; it would give her a chance to question him about dating Cora, and maybe even get a look at his handwriting.

After hanging up with Officer Lewis, Misty immediately called the security system company, sighing with relief when the woman said the installer was back in town and could be at Misty's house within two hours.

"Are you sure you feel safe enough to go back there with a killer out to get you?" Tori asked when Misty called to tell her the news. "You are more than welcome to stay with me until this lunatic is caught."

"I appreciate that, Tori," Misty said with a smile, "but those renovations aren't going to do themselves, and I can't hide away forever. Plus, who knows how long it'll take the police to catch this man when they apparently have no leads."

After going back to Tori's to pick up Wally and their things, Misty met the installer at her house. As she pulled into the driveway, she sat in the car for a moment, reliving everything that had happened last night as she stared up at the old house. A man was murdered inside; how could she possibly live here now with that knowledge?

Because I love this old place.

The thought surprised Misty, and she realized with sudden clarity that it was true. Since her arrival here, she'd somehow grown attached to the creaky floors, high ceilings, gingerbread spindles, and whispers from the past that seemed to emanate from every room. The house fit her like none ever had before, and despite everything that had happened, she was glad to be back.

"Mr. Owens, thank you for coming out so quickly," Misty greeted the installer as she ushered him inside.

"It's no problem at all, ma'am," he said with a friendly smile. "After hearing what happened here last night, I was more than happy to come out and do the job for you."

"It's terrible, isn't it?" Misty shivered as she glanced toward her bedroom door.

Shaking his head, Mr. Owens sighed and said, "It sure is. You know, I haven't been out here since Cora Griffin died, and I'll admit it feels a little strange being out here today."

Tilting her head, Misty asked curiously, "You came out here that night?"

Mr. Owens squatted down to dig around in his bag for some parts, and his tone was a bit distracted as he said, "Yes, ma'am. I worked on the police force for a few years before I got married, so I was one of the men who responded to the phone call that night."

"What phone call?"

Mr. Owens stood up with a small alarm panel in his hand and said, "Mr. Thomas was out taking a walk when he decided to stop by the house for a cup of coffee; apparently he and Cora would sit out on the back porch sometimes at night and visit. When he got to the house, he found Cora's body and immediately ran inside to call us. It was a gruesome sight to be sure."

"Was Officer Lewis working at the station during this time?" she asked, although she already knew the answer.

"He was, but he wasn't working that night," Mr. Owens replied. "In fact, the chief tried to get up with him, but no one seemed to know where he was."

Wrapping her arms around her waist, Misty followed Mr. Owens around the house while he worked, her mind running in a thousand different directions.

"Did *you* think Cora killed herself?" she asked after a moment.

With a sigh, Mr. Owens stopped what he was doing and shook his head. "No, ma'am, I didn't," he said, his tone serious as he turned to look at Misty. "In fact, I tried to convince the chief to investigate further, but when Harlem returned to work a couple of days later, he convinced him otherwise."

"If Officer Lewis didn't even respond to the crime scene, why would he have an opinion about it one way or the other?"

Mr. Owens hesitated, glancing down at the wires in his hand before he said, "Honestly, Miss Raven, I always thought there was more to it than meets the eye. For whatever reason, Harlem didn't want an investigation, and after tying up a few loose ends, the case was closed."

Mr. Owens received a phone call then, and Misty left him alone to get his work done in peace. As she went into the kitchen to fix herself a snack, her mind was filled with everything Mr. Owens had just told her. Where was Officer Lewis the night Cora was killed, and why didn't he want her death to be investigated? It all seemed very suspicious to Misty, and she intended to get to the bottom of it.

That night, Misty set the alarm and made certain that every door and window was securely locked. She didn't like feeling nervous in her own home, and as she settled into bed and turned off the light, she allowed Wally to hop onto the bed next to her, his presence warm and comforting as she drifted off to sleep.

CHAPTER 14

The next morning, Misty drove down to the police station to deliver the note to Officer Lewis. She'd made certain to take a picture of it with her cellphone, in case it got "lost" somehow.

When she arrived at the station, she was taken back to Harlem's large corner office where he ushered her in and asked her to sit down.

"I have a couple of things to talk over with you," he said, closing the door. Turning to look at her, he held out his hand and said, "Did you bring the note?"

Nodding, Misty handed him the note and closely watched his face as he scanned it with his eyes. His expression remained neutral as he moved to sit behind his desk, and Misty wondered all over again at his real reasons for wanting the note.

Placing the note inside his top desk drawer, Officer Lewis cleared his throat and said, "Miss Raven, my partner brought to my attention yesterday that he found a few smudged footprints behind your house during the investigation. He's checking in to it, so I'll be sure to keep you updated."

Leaning forward in her chair with interest, Misty asked, "Does he know what type of shoe it is? And what size?"

"All we know right now is it was a size 12, but we'll know more in a day or so," he replied. "Also, it appears that Loren Thomas doesn't have any living relatives, and since his house is on your property, I'm afraid it's your responsibility to go through his things and dispose of them."

Blinking in surprise, Misty said, "Oh...well, alright." After a brief pause, she asked, "Wasn't Mr. Thomas the one who found Cora's body the night she died?"

Eyeing her with caution, Officer Lewis nodded slowly and said, "Yes. Why?"

Misty shrugged innocently and replied, "I was just wondering why he wasn't investigated."

"He was," Harlem stated, leaning back in his chair and resting his hands on his stomach. "We even checked the upstairs bedroom where Cora was when she...fell, and his fingerprints were nowhere to be found. Loren was just a lonely old man; he was completely harmless."

Misty tilted her head and asked, "Were anyone else's fingerprints found in the upstairs bedroom?"

With a slight sigh of impatience, Officer Lewis said, "Only Cora's, of course, and those belonging to a couple who stayed in the room the previous week. Really, Miss Raven, this amateur detective nonsense of yours is getting a little absurd, don't you think? We did our jobs then, and we're doing them now."

"I'm sure you are; I'm afraid I'm just the curious

type," Misty replied with an innocent smile. Glancing down at her fingernails, she added nonchalantly, "I heard you didn't respond to the call that night."

"It was my night off, and I was…over in Savannah for the weekend," he stated, clearing his throat. "Now, if you don't mind, Miss Raven, I'd like to get back to work."

"Just one more question, if you don't mind," Misty said sweetly.

Officer Lewis rubbed his head and sighed. "Alright, what is it?"

"Were you the secret man that Cora dated?"

Jerking his head up, Officer Lewis stared at Misty in shock, the color leaving his face. "How…how did you find out about that?" he asked in a choked voice. "We kept it a secret; hardly anyone knew."

"Why did you break up?" Misty asked, ignoring his question.

Balling his hands into a tight fist, Harlem looked down at his desk for a moment, and Misty was afraid she'd pushed too far and that he would refuse to answer.

"She was ten years younger than me," he finally said, his tone heavy. "Her grandparents didn't approve, so they forced us to break up and sent her away to college. Because of the age difference, we didn't publicize our relationship, but they caught Cora sneaking out one night to meet me and that was the end of it."

"I'm sorry," Misty said, thoughtfully chewing on her bottom lip as she watched him. By the look on his face and the tone in his voice, he'd loved Cora very much and was devastated to lose her. If Cora felt the same way, why didn't she rekindle the romance when she got home from college? She would have been old enough by then, and her grandparents wouldn't have had a leg to stand on. Apparently, Cora didn't love Harlem the way he loved her, and Misty wondered just how angry he'd been when she returned home and started dating someone else.

"Yes, well, it's all water under the bridge now," Officer Lewis stated, forcing a tight smile.

The phone on his desk rang just then, and Officer Lewis excused himself to answer it. Misty slowly stood to her feet, her eyes scanning his desk for anything with his handwriting on it. She caught a glimpse of an envelope he'd written and laid in the mail basket, and she leaned forward to get a closer look. Harlem spotted her, however, and with a smile, Misty waved goodbye and walked from the room, heaving a sigh of frustration under her breath.

The next afternoon, Misty decided to go back to the library to give the microfilm reader another try. As soon as she walked in, she spotted Jeremy Neely sitting at one of the tables with his laptop computer and went over to speak to him. He seemed very engrossed in his research, and as she stepped up behind him, she glanced over his shoulder to see that he was reading an article on undetectable drugs.

"Doing research for your next mystery book?" she asked, and he jumped in surprise.

Turning to look at her, Jeremy smiled and said, "Oh, it's you, Miss Raven. Yes, the Wi-Fi at my house is down today, and since the coffee shop was crowded, I thought I'd just come here instead."

Nodding her head in the direction of the computer screen, she asked, "Find anything interesting?"

"As a matter of fact, I have," he replied. With a sly grin pulling at his lips, he shook his finger at her and added, "Don't you go tell anyone, though, or my storyline will be spoiled."

Making a show of sealing her lips, Misty smiled and said, "I won't tell a soul."

As she made her way to the microfilm reader, a sudden thought hit her and she paused, her mind whirling. If anyone could concoct a plan for making murder seem like a suicide, it would be a mystery writer. Sinking down into the desk chair, Misty grabbed her phone and searched for a list of his books. Finding his very first one from sixteen years ago, Misty clicked on it and read the synopsis. Her eyes widening, she felt the blood leave her face as she looked up at the man sitting across the room. The storyline was about a young woman who was murdered, but her death was made to look like a suicide.

Misty closed her phone, her thoughts running in a thousand different directions. The book was released a year before Cora's death; was the fact that the story was so similar to Cora's a coincidence, or had he been planning to kill her all along? And why hadn't anyone put the two together?

Jeremy Neely was a very nice man, but Misty decided right then and there that she shouldn't mark him off of her suspect list just yet.

As if he could read her mind, Jeremy glanced up at Misty, and with a slightly awkward smile, she faced the microfilm reader and began her search. She sat there for over two hours, flipping through endless pages of newspapers until she finally decided to give up. As she left the library and headed home, she told herself to stay positive; finding the right information was never easy, and she would just have to keep trying.

That night, as Misty made herself a sandwich for supper, she suddenly heard the distant rumble of thunder. It seemed that a storm was rolling in, and she quickly beckoned Wally to go outside and do his business. While she waited for him on the back porch, she pulled her sweater tighter around herself, the haunting sound of the wind whistling through the pine trees causing her to shiver. Wally bounded through the yard and up the steps to rejoin her on the porch, and she hurriedly ushered him back inside. Storms always put her a bit on edge, and she didn't want to be outside any longer than necessary.

As Misty sat down to eat her sandwich, she could hear the storm moving closer. The wind picked up even more, and the rumbling of thunder was starting to shake the house. Just as she swallowed the last bite of her meal, she thought she heard movement on the back porch. Standing, Misty faced the door, her heart picking up speed. Was she imagining things, or was it possibly just the wind she'd heard? Thinking that she was letting her imagination get the best of her, Misty picked up her plate and walked over to the kitchen sink.

Just then, a scratching sound on the door met Misty's ears, and Wally let out a low growl. Her fingers trembling, Misty turned to look at him just as he lunged at the door, his teeth bared as he began to bark ferociously. The noise continued, and Misty glanced around desperately in search of a weapon, her eyes falling upon a large cutting knife. Grabbing the knife, Misty edged closer to the door, the sound of her heart pounding in her ears nearly drowning out everything else.

"Who…who's there?" she called out, her voice trembling. "I have a weapon."

Suddenly, the lights flickered, just as a mighty boom of thunder reverberated throughout the house. Wally jumped at the door, his mighty paws striking the wood with such force Misty feared it might splinter, and then the scratching stopped.

Running to the window on trembling legs, she looked out to see a large raccoon scurrying across the porch and watched as it disappeared into the darkness.

Sighing with relief, Misty sank down into the kitchen chair, utterly drained as the adrenaline left her body. Wally came to sit by her side and nudged her with his nose; with a smile, Misty leaned over to wrap her arms around him.

"What a good boy you are, guarding the house like that," she said, his soft fur tickling her nose.

The storm continued, and Misty went into her bedroom to get ready for bed. Spotting a folder resting on her bedside table, Misty picked it up, pulled out the pages it held, and began jotting down updates. She'd written out a paper for each suspect in Cora and Hank's deaths, and wanted to add Jeremy's suspicious sounding book to his page.

Glancing through all the pages, she pulled out Rick Harley's; he'd called her earlier with a price to do the plumbing and was supposed to get started tomorrow morning. She was anxious to get a chance to talk with him, and perhaps ask him a few questions.

Her cellphone vibrated just then, and she absently placed the papers back on the table and picked up her phone.

"Are you and Wally surviving the storm okay?"

The text message was from Brice, and Misty smiled at his thoughtfulness.

"Yes, but I'll be glad when it's over," she replied.

They texted for over an hour until the storm had passed, and Misty finally told him they both needed to get some sleep. He said goodnight, and Misty curled up under the covers, not complaining when Wally jumped up beside her. After the excitement of the night, she felt safer with his large body curled next to hers.

CHAPTER 15

Rick Harley and his men arrived early the next morning, and Misty was surprised to see that his brother, Craig, was with them.

"Good morning," she greeted them all. "Craig, I didn't know you worked with your brother."

"I do sometimes," he replied with a smile as he retrieved some equipment from the back of Rick's truck. "Hey, let me know when you're ready for me to start with your orders."

"I will," Misty nodded. "I'm dying to get the swing done, but I think I should have the house and porch painted first."

The men came inside to start in the master bathroom, and Misty fixed them all a cup of coffee.

"I've got some muffins fresh out of the oven, as well, if any of you are interested," Misty told them as she sat the tray of coffee cups on the bathroom counter.

Rick told the men to go get a muffin while he got everything set up, and after they'd all left, Misty decided to grab the opportunity.

"I saw you at the harvest party last weekend," she stated, leaning one hip against the counter. "Did you have a good time?"

With a shrug, Rick said, "Yeah, I guess."

"I noticed that you and Daniel Abraham seemed to be having a bit of an argument, and then you and your wife left early," she continued, watching him intently.

His jaw clenching, Rick cut open the box containing the new bathroom sink and completely ignored Misty's comment. She considered pressing the issue, but could hear his men returning and knew there was no use. With a sigh, she told them to let her know if they needed anything and left them to their work.

With all the work going on in the house, Misty kept Wally tied up on the back porch while she attempted to refurbish an antique sideboard she'd found stashed away in the attic. The weather was nice, and she enjoyed being outside with Wally while she worked. The sideboard was well over one hundred years old and had beautiful carvings around the edges; she couldn't imagine why it had been in the attic and hoped to restore it to its former glory.

After she'd worked for a bit, Misty decided she wanted a bit of music and realized she'd left her phone in the bedroom. She could hear the men moving around upstairs as they worked in one of the guest bathrooms, and she hurried inside to grab her phone. As soon as she entered her bedroom, however, she stopped dead in her tracks and gasped. Rick Harley was standing beside her bed, going through her folder of suspects.

The blood leaving her face, Misty hurried across the room just as Rick spun to face her.

"What do you think you're doing?" she asked, reaching to take the papers from him.

Snatching them away from her, Rick's eyes were filled with anger as he hissed, "Who do you think you are, writing these things about me?" Stepping closer, he grabbed her by the arm in a painful grip and added in a low growl, "And just how did you find out about the blackmail?"

Her heart pounding, Misty struggled to pull away, but his fingers were like iron. "Let me go, Mr. Harley," she begged. "You're hurting me."

Instead of letting go, he tossed the papers aside and grabbed her other arm. His face was a mask of fury as he loomed over her, and before Misty could cry out for help, he pushed her roughly against the wall and said, "I've had just about enough of your meddling, Miss Raven. I think it's high time I put a stop…"

Suddenly, the sound of approaching footsteps echoed through the living room, and Rick quickly let Misty go. He'd just stepped away when his brother entered the room, and Craig paused in the doorway, his expression hesitant when he saw both of their faces.

"Is…everything alright?" he asked slowly.

"Yes," Rick stated, turning a piercing glare on Misty. "Isn't it, Miss Raven?"

When Misty didn't answer, Craig raised his eyebrows and asked, "Misty?"

Rubbing her throbbing arms, Misty nodded her head and said, "Y-yes, everything is fine."

Snatching up both her cellphone and the papers, Misty hurried from the room and into the kitchen, her legs trembling so badly she feared she might faint. She sank down into one of the kitchen chairs and tried to gather her thoughts. Should she call Officer Lewis and tell him she'd been threatened? *He's already accused me of stirring up too much trouble,* she thought with a sigh. *He'll rake me over the coals if he finds out I have a folder filled with suspects lying around my house.*

Whether she went to Officer Lewis with this or not, she certainly didn't want Rick Harley working in her house any longer. How would she ever go about getting rid of him, though?

Before she could come to any decisions, she heard the front door slam and then the revving of a truck engine as it drove away from the house. She'd just stood up to go investigate when a light knock sounded on the kitchen door.

"Misty?" Craig popped his head into the room. "Can I come in?"

"Of course," Misty replied with a nod.

Stepping into the kitchen, Craig pushed his hands into the pockets of his pants and said in a slightly awkward tone, "Rick just left. He said to tell you that he won't be back and I'm in charge now." Clearing his throat, he stepped closer and added, "Misty, I hate to pry, but would you mind telling me what's happened? I thought I heard Rick say something about blackmail before I walked into the room."

Hesitating, Misty wondered if she should tell Craig. He'd always been very kind to her and she didn't want to upset him, but she knew it wasn't her place to be spreading rumors.

"I…recently uncovered something, and your brother accidentally stumbled upon some notes I'd left in my bedroom. I'm sorry, Craig, but that's all I can say. I'm afraid you'll have to ask your brother," she finally said with a sigh.

"I understand," he replied, nodding. "Listen, will it be okay if I continue with the job, or would you prefer to hire someone else? I've helped Rick on many occasions and his men are really good at their jobs, but I'll understand if you want to find another company."

"I would greatly appreciate it if you would stay and finish the job," Misty replied with a grateful smile. "Thank you, Craig."

"You're very welcome," he said warmly. "It will probably take at least another day, maybe two, until we finish, but we'll do our best to hurry."

He turned to leave the room, but hesitated. Turning back to face Misty, he cleared his throat and said, "Maybe you, me, Tori, and Brice could go out this Friday night? I hear they're playing old Humphrey Bogart movies at the theater all weekend, and we could get something to eat afterward."

"Sounds fun to me," Misty replied, although she

wasn't sure how Brice would feel about going out with Craig. "Why don't you ask Tori and I'll ask Brice and we'll go from there?"

His face filling with pleasure, Craig nodded eagerly and said, "I'll do that."

After he'd gone, Misty sat down at the table and texted Tori, just to give her a heads up about the invitation. She couldn't tell exactly how her friend felt about Craig, and she didn't want Tori to be uncomfortable or feel forced into accepting.

"It doesn't matter either way to me," Misty told her. *"Also, I have some interesting news to share about his brother whenever you get a chance to talk."*

Shoving the phone into her pocket, Misty grabbed her suspect folder and put it in the back of her pantry behind the cereal. The last thing she needed was for another one of the workers to find it and cause an uproar.

After grabbing a quick snack, she went back outside and returned to her work, a chill creeping up her spine as she thought of the encounter with Rick Harley. If Craig hadn't come in, Misty wasn't sure what Rick was planning to do, and she decided right then and there to steer clear of him from now on.

A couple of hours later, Misty went inside to fix herself some lunch, and quickly realized she was out of lunch meat and didn't wish to dirty up the kitchen making anything from scratch. Deciding to run into town to do a bit of much needed grocery shopping, Misty quickly changed her clothes and told Craig that she was going out for a bit.

By the time Misty was nearly done shopping, her buggy was filled to the brim, and she still hadn't gotten any lunch meat. Heading toward the deli, she rounded the corner and nearly ran right over Mr. Donovan, Tori's old schoolteacher.

"Oh, Mr. Donovan, I'm so sorry. Are you alright?" she gasped just as her buggy came into contact with his hip.

"I'm quite alright," he stated with a chuckle as he began to rub his hip. "Maybe the store should consider putting bells on their carts."

Smiling sheepishly, Misty said, "That's not such a bad idea, or maybe I should just slow down and watch where I'm going."

Mr. Donovan glanced into her cart and, his eyes lighting up, he pointed to the box of homemade peanut brittle and said, "Those are my favorites. One of our locals, Mrs. Henderson, makes them. I hope you left me a box?"

"Yes, I did," Misty said, smiling. A thought struck her just then and, clearing her throat, she asked, "Mr. Donovan, do you remember when the Spanish teacher and her students went missing about twenty-five years ago?"

Blinking in surprise, Mr. Donovan nodded and said, "Why, yes, I do. I was teaching at the elementary school at the time."

"Do you remember anything about the Spanish teacher? Tori's family was telling me about what happened a couple of weeks ago, and I thought the teacher's story sounded a bit vague."

Misty could see the curiosity in Mr. Donovan's eyes, but was relieved when he didn't ask any questions.

"Well, let me see," he said, resting his arm against his belly as he tapped his chin thoughtfully. "I believe her first name was Elena, but I can't remember her last name. It might still be in the school's records, but I don't know if they'll give you any information unless you're a relative."

"I understand," Misty replied with a nod. "Do you remember if Elena and her husband had any children?"

Biting his bottom lip, Mr. Donovan pondered the question with squinted eyes for a moment. "You know what?" he finally said, his face brightening. "I almost think I *do* remember that they had a child. I'm afraid I can't remember if it was a girl or boy, though, or even how old it was."

"Don't you think it's odd how they all disappeared and no one knows what happened to any of them?" Misty asked.

"Yes, I certainly do," he replied. Glancing around, Mr. Donovan lowered his voice and added, "Our police force isn't the best, in my opinion, and I always thought they did a poor job of investigating the disappearances of those girls."

"Did the families ever go to the FBI or anything?"

"They tried, but never got anywhere," he replied

with a sigh. "Since the girls supposedly left behind a goodbye note, they said there wasn't much they could do. They looked in to it for a little while, but other cases took precedence and they eventually just fell through the cracks. I believe that one family had enough money to hire a private detective, but he couldn't find out anything either."

"How strange," Misty muttered, her mind whirling.

"If I didn't know any better, I'd say you were a journalist looking for a good story," Mr. Donovan said with a slight smile, eyeing Misty closely.

Before Misty could reply, a woman in her mid-fifties called out, "Yoohoo, Patrick Donovan, I thought that was you!"

Misty quickly excused herself and hurried away, grateful for the interruption. She wasn't ready to tell anyone her reasons for asking so many questions, but knew the truth would come out eventually.

CHAPTER 16

When Misty finally arrived back home, the sun was going down and Craig and his men were gone. She'd just finished unloading her groceries when her cellphone chimed, and she looked to see that Tori had answered her text message from earlier that afternoon.

"I'm sorry it took so long to reply," she said. *"My stove broke down around noon and I had to get someone out here to repair it. Now that it's finally fixed, I've got to do all the baking for in the morning; I'll be out here until who knows when. Oh, the joys of running your own business!"*

"I'll come by to help you," Misty texted back. *"Be there in ten minutes."*

After quickly feeding Wally, Misty hurried out to her car and headed back into town. Nearly everything was closed down for the night, and the streetlights illuminated Main Street in a warm, cozy glow. As Misty parked in front of the coffee shop and climbed from her car, she glanced down the street and noticed that Daniel Abraham's café lights were still on.

I guess Tori isn't the only one working late, she thought as she hurried around to the back door and knocked.

"Thank you so much for coming," Tori said when she opened the door and ushered Misty inside. Her hair was pulled up into a messy bun, and she had flour all over her apron. "You are a lifesaver."

"I'm happy to help," Misty said with a smile as she tied on one of Tori's extra aprons.

The two immediately got to work making muffins, pastries, and scones for the next day, and as Misty mixed the dough for Tori's wonderful pecan pie muffins, she told her friend about the altercation with Rick Harley.

Tori stopped what she was doing to stare at Misty with wide eyes. "Misty, he threatened you!" she cried, a bit of batter dripping from the spoon she held. "Did you report it to the police?"

Misty shook her head and sighed. "No, I was afraid Officer Lewis would only accuse me of causing more trouble."

"Well, I think he should know about it," Tori continued to protest. "Rick actually grabbed your arm and pushed you against the wall? This is serious, Misty! I'm so glad Craig intervened."

"So am I," Misty replied as she scooped the muffin batter into the trays. "Speaking of Craig, what do you think about the four of us going out this weekend? He mentioned it, and I thought I would ask you about it."

"Oh, I don't know," Tori said with a worried sigh. "It's basically a double date, and I don't know how I feel about going on a date with Craig."

"It's not a double date because Brice and I aren't dating," Misty stated matter-of-factly.

"Well, it *seems* like a double date," Tori said, her blue eyes sparkling. "And I would personally be thrilled if you and Brice really did start dating."

"Tori, I don't even know if I'm going to stay in Shady Pines permanently," Misty said as she put the muffin trays in the oven. "So, I don't need to get involved with anyone."

Her eyebrows raised, Tori planted her hands on her hips and asked, "What do you mean you don't know if you're staying?"

"I've never stayed in one place for very long," Misty replied with a shrug. "I move from town to town renovating old homes to sell them; it's just what I do."

Pursing her lips, Tori crossed her arms and said, "Well, I think you should stay. Once you finish renovating the old Griffin house, you can turn it back into a bed-and-breakfast. People used to love to stay there when it was open!"

"Oh, I don't know," Misty said. "I know nothing about running a bed-and-breakfast."

Grabbing a couple of cartons full of eggs from the refrigerator, Tori handed one to Misty and kept one for herself. "Misty," she said, touching her friend gently on the arm, "you've been searching for a home for so long, and I truly believe you've found it. You and that house fit together like two peas in a pod, my whole family adores you, and I know you'd come to love it here if you tried."

"Your family might like me, but few others around here do," Misty snickered.

"That's just because they haven't gotten to know you," Tori stated as she cracked four eggs into a mixing bowl. With a cocked eyebrow, she added in a mischievous tone, "I'm pretty sure Adam Dawson likes you, and he's not related to me at all."

Laughing, Misty threw up her hands and said, "Alright, alright. I'll think about staying. Are you satisfied?"

"Yes!" Tori squealed, clapping her hands in excitement.

The two continued to work and chat, and before Misty knew it, everything was finished and it was time to clean up. After washing all the dishes, putting away the baked goods until morning, scrubbing the kitchen counters, and sweeping the floor, it was almost midnight.

"I'd have been here until daybreak if you hadn't come," Tori said with a grateful smile as she walked Misty out. "Thank you so much for all of your help."

As soon as they stepped out the front door, Misty glanced down the street and noticed that while Daniel Abraham's café lights were off, the light from his office window beamed brightly.

"Is he normally up so late?" she asked, motioning toward the café.

Tori shook her head. "No, the downstairs lights are always out when I leave here at night. He's probably just getting something from his office."

"I think we should go over and check on him," Misty stated, the feeling that something wasn't right boosting her to step forward as she hurriedly crossed the street.

"Misty, have you lost your mind?" Tori cried as she ran after her. "We can't go barging in there this time of night!"

"Something doesn't feel right, Tori," Misty insisted as they neared the café and began circling around to the rear entrance. "Don't come with me if you don't want to."

"I can't believe we're doing this," Tori muttered.

The back of the building was shrouded in darkness, with only one small light above the door. Misty stepped up and raised her hand to knock, stopping when she noticed the door stood slightly ajar. With a frown, she pushed the door open and poked her head inside, her eyes squinting as she tried to see through the shadows.

"Misty, what are you doing?" Tori hissed from behind as she grabbed at Misty's arm.

Daniel's office was just down the hall; Misty could see the light drifting from under the door. She stepped further into the building and opened her mouth to call out, but froze when a sudden *thud* from inside the office broke the silence.

"What was that?" Tori gasped as she hurried in behind Misty.

Motioning for her to be quiet, Misty grabbed Tori's hand and began creeping quietly down the hall toward the office. Misty could hear grunts and movement coming from inside the room, and as they drew nearer, her foot suddenly landed on a loose floorboard and the loud *creak* that followed sounded loud enough to wake the dead. The two girls froze, their hearts pounding as the sounds from inside of the office stopped. Gathering her courage, Misty reached out to clasp the doorknob, ready to throw it open and find out what was going on, when all of the sudden, the door was yanked from her hand and a large shadow bounded from the room.

Before Misty could utter a sound, she was shoved roughly to the floor, her knee striking the wood painfully as she fell. With a scream, Tori jumped back just as the intruder ran past them and out the back door, his presence sweeping from the building like a strong wind. Her heart pounding, Misty tried to see who it was, but failed; it was too dark, and he was dressed all in black.

"Misty, are you alright?" Tori cried as she reached down to help her up.

"Y-yes," Misty nodded.

Ignoring the throbbing in her knee, she stepped around the corner to enter the office, blinking as she tried to adjust her eyes to the sudden bright light. Tori stepped in behind her and both women stopped dead in their tracks, gasping at the sight before them. Lying on the floor beside his desk was Daniel Abraham, and it was apparent by the bloody gash in his throat and blank, glazed over expression in his eyes that he wouldn't see the light of another day.

With trembling fingers, Misty immediately called the police, and the two women waited on pins and needles for them to show up. Tori locked the office door, just in case the murderer decided to come back, and while they waited, Misty slowly walked around the room, being careful not to disturb anything. The office was a mess; Daniel's chair was overturned, his computer lay smashed on the floor, and papers were strewn everywhere.

"I-I hope the police will hurry," Tori said in a trembling voice as she wrapped her arms protectively around her waist.

Chewing on her bottom lip, Misty walked around Daniel's desk and, pulling her sweater over her fingertips, opened the top middle drawer to look inside.

"Misty, what are you doing?" Tori gasped.

"It's gone," Misty said, looking up at her friend with wide eyes. "The box with the blackmail papers is gone."

"Maybe Daniel put it somewhere else," Tori replied.

Suddenly, the light reflected off of something that was partially hidden under the desk, and Misty bent down to pick it up.

"Tori," Misty said, holding it up for her friend to

see, "this is Officer Lewis's pen."

"How do you know that?" Tori asked, her brow wrinkling.

"He always keeps it in his shirt pocket," Misty stated, walking around the desk to show Tori. "And look, it has his initials engraved on it."

"But why would his pen be under Daniel's desk?" Tori wanted to know.

Before Misty could reply, the police arrived, and she hurriedly let them in. She was anxious to ask Officer Lewis about his pen but was surprised to find that his partner, Officer Dylan Mitchell, and an ambulance were the only ones to show up.

"A forensics team is on the way," Dylan said as he and the EMT hurried inside.

"Where is Officer Lewis?" Misty questioned.

"Tonight is his night off," he replied.

The forensics team arrived shortly after, and Misty and Tori were asked to wait outside while they investigated the crime scene.

"I can't believe this is happening," Tori said, tears filling her eyes as she sank down into one of the restaurant chairs. "I've known Mr. Abraham for years, and now he's dead."

Misty went to her friend's side and wrapped a supportive arm around her shoulders. "I'm sorry, Tori," she said gently. "I'm a little shaken up myself after discovering a dead body and coming so close to the murderer."

"Why don't you stay with me tonight?" Tori asked, wiping her eyes with the back of her hand.

"It's so late, and I think we could both use the company."

Misty agreed, and while the forensics team worked, Dylan came out to question the two women. Misty told him everything, from the time she arrived at Tori's coffee shop to the moment they stepped inside the office and found Mr. Abraham's dead body.

"Officer Mitchell," Misty said, clearing her throat, "I've…heard a rumor that Mr. Abraham was blackmailing Rick Harley."

Glancing up at Misty in surprise, Dylan said, "*What?*"

"Rick was working at my house earlier today, and he all but admitted it."

"*And* he threatened Misty," Tori spoke up.

"I will definitely look into this," Dylan said, reaching up to loosen his collar. He looked to be in his early thirties, with a buzz cut and striking hazel eyes. Misty had heard that he spent several years in the military, and she wondered why he'd decided to come back and settle here.

"I also found this lying on the floor half-hidden under Mr. Abraham's desk," Misty said, handing Dylan the pen. "Doesn't it belong to Officer Lewis?"

His brow lowering, Dylan studied the pen for a moment without answering. "Yes, it does," he finally muttered. Clearing his throat, he looked back up at Misty and Tori and said, "Well, I think that's all the questions I have for tonight. If I need anything else, I'll give y'all a call."

By the time Misty and Tori got to Tori's house, it was almost two o'clock in the morning and both girls were exhausted. Tori loaned Misty a pair of pajamas, and after taking a quick shower, Misty settled down in the guest bedroom and tried to get some sleep. All she could think about, however, were the events of the night, and just before she drifted off to sleep, she wondered once again why Officer Lewis's pen was under Daniel Abraham's desk.

CHAPTER 17

The next day, the whole town was in an uproar. Daniel Abraham had been a beloved citizen his whole life, and everyone wanted his killer caught. The front page of the newspaper was filled with pictures of Daniel and the story of what happened, and all throughout the day, Misty relived it over and over in her mind. When Officer Lewis called and asked that Misty and Tori come down to the station for further questioning, she was glad to have the chance to talk to him about it.

"Miss Raven, Miss Barlow," he said once they'd arrived at the station and were seated across from his desk. "I'd like to know why the two of you were at the café last night when Daniel Abraham was killed?"

The two took turns explaining, and once they'd finished, Officer Lewis leaned his elbows over on the desk and interlaced his fingers. "Ladies, I'm sure you must know how odd all of that sounds, and in my opinion, it isn't quite adding up," he stated with a sniff. Cocking an eyebrow at Misty, he added, "And what a coincidence that *you* happened to be around once again while another catastrophe was taking place."

"*She* might have been around, but *you* certainly weren't, were you?" Tori spoke up, and Misty glanced at her friend in surprise. "Did Dylan mention we found your pen under Daniel Abraham's desk?"

Misty watched as the color drained from Harlem's face, and sitting back to fidget awkwardly in his chair, he cleared his throat and said, "Yes, as a matter of fact, he did. I...must have dropped it when I spoke with Daniel last week about...about a traffic ticket he failed to pay."

"The pen was in your pocket when I saw you earlier this week," Misty stated matter-of-factly.

His eyes narrowing, Officer Lewis said in a low, steely voice, "If you two are trying to accuse me of something, why don't you just say so? I don't think a pen is enough evidence to hold up in court, though, do you?"

He was being very smug, and it rankled Misty. Before she could stop herself, she raised her chin and snapped, "Don't worry, Officer, we won't accuse you of anything unless more evidence happens to be uncovered. May I suggest you do the same? Because I don't think this little invitation to be questioned like two criminals was necessary. Everything happened just as we said, and it's not our fault that Daniel Abraham is dead."

Harlem didn't say anything for a moment; he simply sat there glaring at Misty with a clenched jaw. Finally, he forced a tight smile and, motioning to the door, said, "You're free to go."

Nodding, Tori and Misty stood to leave, but before she exited the room, Misty glanced back at

Harlem and asked, "By the way, did any more information come in about the shoe prints found outside of my house?"

With jerky movements, Officer Lewis began gathering up some papers and said stiffly, "All we know is the man was wearing a pair of those sneaker type boots."

"Thank you."

With that, the two left the station, and as soon as they reached the parking lot, Tori put her hands on her hips and said, "That man has a lot of nerve! I can't believe he was so rude to you."

"Thanks for taking up for me," Misty said with a grateful smile as she linked her arm through Tori's and they began walking toward their cars. "He *is* rather infuriating, but I guess I can't blame him. It seems that I have a knack for being in the wrong place at the wrong time."

"Well, none of this is your fault, and I don't appreciate his attitude," Tori stated with a sniff.

"Did you notice the look on his face when you mentioned the pen?" Misty asked. "I don't think Dylan really did tell him about it."

"I don't either," Tori replied, digging her car keys from her purse. "He looked completely shocked and then stumbled around trying to think of an excuse for why it was there."

They'd just reached their cars when Misty's cellphone rang, and she groaned when she saw it was Craig and realized he must be at the house ready to work and couldn't get inside.

"I forgot all about him," she muttered under her breath as she answered the phone. "Craig, I'm so sorry! I'll be there in ten minutes."

"Is everything okay?" he asked.

Waving goodbye to Tori, Misty jumped into her car and quickly backed out of the parking space. "Did you hear what happened last night?" she asked him as she drove away from the station.

"To Mr. Abraham? Yes, I did," he replied with a sigh. "It's just terrible."

Misty wanted to ask him if he knew where his brother was the night before, but didn't dare.

"Tori and I went over to check on him and we sort of bumped into the killer," she said, proceeding to tell him everything that happened.

"Misty, that could have been very dangerous," he exclaimed. "Are you and Tori alright?"

Misty pulled up in front of her house and parked, smiling and waving to Craig as she hung up the phone and got out. "We're both fine," she said as she walked toward him.

"Did y'all see who the killer was?" Craig asked as Misty let him and his men inside.

"No, unfortunately not," she replied. "We did, however, find Officer Lewis's pen under Daniel's desk, which I think is a bit strange."

"Maybe he dropped it the day before last when he stopped by the café to see Mr. Abraham," Craig stated as his men began bringing in the supplies from the work truck.

"You saw him there?" Misty asked.

Craig nodded. "Yes, I stopped by to grab a to-go order, and while I waited, I saw Harlem come out of Mr. Abraham's office. He looked a little upset, if you ask me, and slammed the door when he left."

"I wonder what they could have been arguing about?" Misty asked, her brow furrowing.

"Who knows?" Craig shrugged. "Harlem is known to be a bit short-tempered every now and then."

Craig's men were ready to get to work, and Misty headed to the kitchen to see about Wally while they went upstairs to pick back up where they left off.

"Hey, you," she greeted her dog as he bounded to her side and happily bumped against her leg. "Did you miss me last night?"

As Misty let Wally outside and fixed his food, her mind wandered back to the conversation with Craig, and she couldn't help but feel curious about what Daniel Abraham had done to make Harlem so upset. Everyone around town sang Daniel's praises, but it seemed to Misty that he hadn't been quite the saint everyone made him out to be. Had Harlem found out about the blackmail, and confronted Daniel? Perhaps that's why the papers in Daniel's desk were gone...or perhaps Rick Harley killed him and took the papers.

With a sigh, Misty shook her head in frustration and made herself a cup of coffee. Things just kept getting more and more confusing, and Misty wished she could figure out what it all meant.

Friday night, Misty met Tori, Craig, and Brice at a small pizza parlor, the only other restaurant in town that was open. It felt a bit strange to be out having a good time with everything that had happened, but Misty and Tori felt it would do them both good.

As they sat down to enjoy their pizza in the cozy, old-fashioned style restaurant with soft music playing in the background and string lights dangling overhead, Misty noticed how quiet Brice was and how Tori kept chattering on as if nervous or uncomfortable. Craig was a bit awkward, and Misty winced when he almost knocked his drink over. When Adam stepped inside, she smiled and waved, grateful for the distraction.

"Hello, everyone," he greeted them with a friendly smile.

"Here alone?" Misty asked, tucking a stray tendril behind one ear. She'd worn her hair up to compliment the red turtleneck sweater she'd chosen from her closet, and as she propped her hand under her chin and looked up at Adam, she didn't realize how striking she looked.

Adam nodded, shoving his hands into his pockets. "Yes, ma'am. I didn't feel like cooking tonight, so I thought I'd drop by and grab a pizza."

"Why don't you join us?" Misty asked, ignoring the frown Brice threw her way as she scooted over to make room for Adam. "We have plenty of pizza. Don't we, y'all?"

Tori seemed equally grateful for Adam's presence and eagerly nodded her head. "Yes, absolutely. We'd love it if you joined us, Adam."

"Alright, if you insist," Adam stated with a grin as he slid into the booth next to Misty.

Not sensing any tension at all, Adam began talking about work and the weather, and pretty soon, everyone began to loosen up and enjoy themselves. The men, especially Adam and Brice, raced to tell the best story or funniest joke, and Misty and Tori were in tears with laughter by the time the pizza was gone and their stomachs full.

"If we don't want to miss the beginning of the movie, we'd better go," Craig spoke up, glancing at his watch.

Nodding their heads in agreement, everyone tossed some tip money onto the table and hurried to the theater. When they arrived, Misty was surprised to find that the place was almost full.

"I didn't realize many people still watched old movies," she stated as they all walked inside.

"They're probably here for the popcorn," Brice said with a wry grin as he pointed to the "free popcorn" sign at the entrance.

They found their seats, and Misty had to keep herself from rolling her eyes when Brice quickly claimed the only available seat beside her, as Tori had taken the other.

"If you're going to sit there, we have to have an

understanding," Misty told him, her voice low.

Raising his eyebrows, Brice asked, "And what would that be?"

With a mischievous glint in her eyes, she pointed to the armrest between them and said, "This is *my* armrest."

"I thought maybe we could share it," he replied with a wink.

Laughing, Misty shook her head and turned to Tori when her friend elbowed her.

"I keep forgetting to ask, but would you like to join my family for Thanksgiving next Thursday?" Tori asked. "We'd really love to have you."

Her heart warming at the request, Misty nodded her head and said, "I would love to come. What can I bring?"

"Oh, just bring a dessert or something simple," Tori replied with a wave of her hand. "Mom insists on getting up at the crack of dawn to prepare a huge feast for everyone, and she refuses to let anyone help. I always take a pan of biscuits, but that's all she lets me do."

Laughing, Misty said, "Okay, a simple dessert it is then."

The movie was about to start when Craig announced he wanted a bag of Doritos, and as he hurried off to get them, Brice leaned closer to Misty and muttered, "The guy is on a date and he wants Doritos? Those will do wonders for his breath, plus make a mess."

"Stop being so hard on him," Misty scolded with

a sigh. "He's just nervous."

"Misty, how are the renovations going?" Adam spoke up, leaning around Brice to smile at her.

Ignoring the look of irritation on Brice's face at the interruption, Misty met Adam's piercing black gaze and said, "It's going a bit slower than I'd like, but once Craig and his men get the plumbing done, I think I'll start to feel more accomplished."

"Rick Harley isn't doing it?" Adam asked, his brow furrowing.

Before Misty could answer, Craig returned, and the lights dimmed as the movie started. While she watched the black and white scenes flash before her, Misty thought of Mr. Sikes, the old man who was so much like a grandfather to her before he died, and she remembered the many times they'd watched these types of old movies together. He'd loved them; he always said they reminded him of the days when he was young, and Misty felt her chest squeeze. She missed him so much; he'd been the only real family she'd ever had, but her heart was warmed by Tori's invitation to join her family for Thanksgiving. She'd never experienced a holiday with a real family before, and she was excited to join the Barlows this year.

The movie had just ended and everyone was exiting the theater when Craig's cellphone rang. While Tori, Brice, and Adam chatted about the movie, Misty watched Craig's face and immediately knew something was wrong.

Craig ended the call and put the cellphone back

into his pocket, his face as white as a ghost.

"Craig, is everything alright?" Misty asked when he rejoined their group.

"That…that was Rick," he said, pausing to run his fingers through his hair as he attempted to get his thoughts in order.

Tori gently reached out to touch Craig's arm. "Craig, what's wrong?" she asked, her voice filled with concern. "Has something happened?"

He stared at her for a moment, as if not really seeing her, until finally he said in a choked voice, "He's at the police station. He's…he's been arrested for the murder of Daniel Abraham."

CHAPTER 18

For the next few days, all anyone could talk about was Rick Harley's arrest. Some said they weren't surprised, that they'd never cared for Rick's negative attitude and cynicism, while others were shocked.

"I know he's not the nicest person in the world," Mrs. Whitlock, the owner of the beauty salon, said, "but I never would have thought he was capable of **murder**! I mean, I've known the man my whole life."

"I heard Daniel was blackmailing Rick," another lady in the salon spoke up, "but I don't know what for."

By the time Thanksgiving Day arrived, there were so many stories and rumors circulating throughout the town that Misty didn't know what to believe.

"Don't look so sad," Misty told Wally as she prepared to leave for the Barlow's house. "I'll bring you back a turkey leg or something; I promise."

When Misty arrived at Mr. and Mrs. Barlow's house, everyone else was already there, and she hurried inside with her homemade buttermilk pie.

"I figured Mrs. Barlow made a pumpkin pie, and since I'm not much of a cook, I thought that this would be the safest option," Misty told Tori with a laugh as her friend welcomed her into the house.

"We all love buttermilk pie," Tori exclaimed with excitement as she took the pie from Misty. "Would you mind helping me set the table? We're running a bit behind, and Mom is having a fit."

With a chuckle, Misty nodded and followed her friend into the dining room, where they quickly began to set the table. Mr. Neil, Pop, and Brice were in the living room watching the football game, and Misty shook her head when their yells emanated throughout the house.

"Will we be able to tear them away when everything is ready?" Misty asked, nodding her head toward the men.

"Oh, yes," Tori nodded with a laugh. "If there's anything they love more than watching football, it's eating."

Her words were proven correct, for when all of the food rested on the table and Mrs. Amy announced it was time to eat, all three men hurried from the living room with rumbling bellies and excitement in their eyes.

"This looks amazing, Aunt Amy," Brice exclaimed as he kissed his aunt on the cheek.

Misty couldn't help but agree with him; a steaming hot turkey sat in the middle of the table and was accompanied by cornbread dressing, sweet potato soufflé, creamed corn, macaroni and cheese, butter peas, and fresh, fluffy biscuits. It all smelled amazing, and Misty couldn't wait to try everything.

After saying a prayer of thanks, everyone dug in, and the room was immediately filled with chatter and the clinking of silverware. Misty kept quiet for a few moments and just soaked it all in; the warm, cozy feeling of love and familiarity that can only exist within a family, the laughter and jokes, and the feeling of comfort and "home". She'd never felt anything like it before and found herself wishing once again for a family of her own.

"Misty, did Craig and his men finish with the plumbing?" Brice asked as he helped himself to another biscuit.

"Yes, he did," she replied with a nod. "I really didn't expect him to with…well, everything that's going on, but he said that he needed to keep busy, so I didn't protest."

"Poor thing," Mrs. Amy said with a sigh. "I can't imagine how hard this must be on Rick's family."

"I wonder what Daniel was blackmailing him about?" Pop spoke up as he passed Mr. Neil the corn.

"Who knows if we'll ever find out the whole truth," Tori said.

"Why do you think his wife hasn't paid the bail money?" Brice questioned, his brow furrowed.

"She's probably glad to be rid of the old grump," Mr. Neil stated with a chuckle.

"Neil," Mrs. Amy scolded him. "Maybe they don't have the money."

"Craig wouldn't have enough to bail him out?"

Misty spoke up.

"Craig has never really had a steady job," Pop said. "He's done a bit with his woodworking business, but not enough to be able to afford to bail his brother out. He's had to work with Rick just to keep his head above water."

"And Rick lets him know it every chance he gets," Mr. Neil said, shaking his head. "Poor Craig has had to live under his older brother's overbearing shadow for so long that I don't know how he's coped."

"He should have been a man and stood up to Rick years ago," Brice stated.

"Be nice," Tori said, slapping her cousin lightly on the arm.

"Oh, sorry, I forgot I was talking about your boyfriend," Brice said with a grin.

"What's this?" Tori's parents asked in unison, their eyebrows raised in surprise.

Blushing, Tori sighed and said, "He's not my boyfriend."

"But he wants to be."

Shooting a glare at Brice, Tori stated, "Well, he's **not,** so let's just leave it at that, shall we?"

Seeing the need to change the subject, Misty quickly stepped in and said, "So, Mr. Neil, how is Trampas?"

His face beaming proudly, Mr. Neil said, "Just marvelous. I've decided to breed him."

The conversation flowed smoothly from there, and before Misty knew it, everyone's plates were cleaned and it was time for dessert. Knowing that Misty was going to bring a dessert, Mrs. Amy only made one pie, and she brought both to the table while Misty helped Tori bring out the dessert plates.

"Mrs. Amy, that pumpkin pie looks absolutely delicious," Misty told her hostess.

Touching Misty lightly on the arm, Mrs. Amy smiled and said, "Thank you, dear, so does your pie. I'm so glad you joined us tonight."

Warmed by her kindness, Misty said, "Thank you for having me."

Both pies were a success, and within twenty minutes, there were only crumbs left in the bottom of the pans, and everyone was complaining about eating too much.

"I'll help Misty clear the table, Aunt Amy, while you and Tori do the dishes," Brice offered when the women stood to clean up.

Mr. Neil and Pop went out to the barn while Tori and her mother went into the kitchen, leaving Misty and Brice alone.

"It was very nice of you to help clean up," Misty told him as she began stacking the plates on top of one another.

"What can I say?" Brice asked with a twinkle in his eye as he picked up the stack of dishes to carry into the kitchen. "I'm a very nice guy."

"Humble, too," Misty laughed.

The two of them went back and forth to the kitchen carrying the dirty dishes and plates for Tori and Mrs. Amy to clean, and before long, the table was bare and Misty grabbed a wet cloth to wipe it off with.

"Have you gotten a chance to clean out Mr. Thomas's cabin yet?" Brice asked as he leaned against the server and watched her.

Misty shook her head. "No, I keep putting it off," she said, scrunching up her face. "It feels so weird to clean out someone else's house, especially someone I barely knew."

Crossing his ankles, Brice stuffed his hands into his pockets and said, "I know what you mean. If you want, I could come out on Saturday to help you; we could probably get it done in a couple of days."

"Really?" Misty asked, glancing at him in surprise. "That would be great, Brice. Thank you."

They made plans to start at ten o'clock, and then Misty went into the kitchen to help Tori and Mrs. Amy finish up while Brice joined Mr. Neil and Pop in the barn. By the time everything was cleaned and put away, it was nearly six o'clock.

"Tori, go call the men back inside," Mrs. Amy said as she untied her apron. "It's time for charades."

Smiling with excitement, Tori nodded and hurried to the back door. "It's tradition," she told Misty. "You'll stay, won't you?"

Misty had never played charades before, and the game that quickly got underway had her laughing so hard she was in tears. The three women formed a team against the men, and just watching Pop pretending to be a rooster or Brice acting like a ballerina made her laugh even harder.

It was nearly the end of the game, and both teams were tied. Misty was up next, and she nervously took her place at the front of the room. The action she was to perform was "falling off a bike", and when Brice called out that the timer was ready, she dove into the performance at full throttle. She nearly threw her back out in the process, but when Tori called out the right answer, Misty jumped up and squealed with delight.

"Were you once a professional stuntman?" Brice asked, shaking his head as he laughed.

"You're not a sore loser, are you?" Misty winked at him.

They all sat down then and listened to Tori and Mr. Neil as they played the piano and sang a duet, and when it was finally time to go, Misty was sad to leave. She'd had a wonderful time, and if she eventually had to leave this town just like every other, she would cherish the memory of her time here forever.

After thanking Tori and her mother once again for inviting her over, Misty said her goodbyes and headed home…with an extra bone from the turkey in a paper bag for Wally, just as she'd promised.

CHAPTER 19

When Saturday arrived, Misty got up early so she would be ready when Brice came at ten to help her with Mr. Thomas's cabin. When she awoke, she realized with dismay that her phone had crashed during the night and was dead. She tried for an hour to get it turned back on, but soon realized it was hopeless and she'd have to go into town on Monday to get a new one.

After feeding Wally and fixing herself a bowl of cereal, Misty changed her clothes, pulled her hair up into a high ponytail, and was ready and waiting for Brice at ten o'clock sharp. When thirty minutes passed and he didn't show up, she assumed he must have forgotten and decided to go out to the cabin without him. As she grabbed several boxes and left the house, she decided to leave a note on the front door just in case he showed up late, and then jumped into her car and headed out to the road.

The morning was dark and dreary, and she had to drive slowly as she searched for the small driveway she'd seen before that led to Mr. Thomas's cabin. When she finally found it, she turned down the narrow, bumpy road and clicked on her headlights to better see through the heavy, dark trees. In the short time that passed since Mr.

Thomas's death, weeds and shrubs had already started to take over the driveway, and Misty had to drive carefully so as not to scratch her car.

Finally, Misty arrived at the cabin, and as she climbed from her car and retrieved the boxes from her backseat, she glanced up at the sky, taking in the thick, gray clouds overhead. A cold breeze whistled through the trees and blew Misty's ponytail around her shoulders, and she fought off a shiver as she hurried into the small house.

Floorboards creaked beneath her feet as she slowly walked around the dark cabin, feeling a little overwhelmed as she tried to decide where to begin. Thankfully, the cabin was small and Mr. Thomas apparently was a "less is more" kind of man, but after living in a place for so long, a person was bound to accumulate some things. With a sigh, Misty clicked on a few lights and decided to begin in the bedroom.

Brice kneeled beside his truck and shook his head with frustration as he surveyed the flat tire. He was already running late, and it would take at least thirty minutes to change the tire. Sighing, he pulled out his cellphone and dialed Misty's number; he'd texted her this morning and received no answer, so he thought perhaps she would answer a phone call.

When the call went straight to voicemail, Brice

began to feel a bit concerned. Stuffing his phone back into his pocket, he quickly began changing the tire, feeling anxious to get to Misty's house and find out why she wasn't answering.

He'd just finished with the tire when his phone rang, and with a sigh of relief, he pulled it from his pocket to answer.

"Hey, it's Tori," his cousin said on the other end, and he felt his stomach sink. He'd thought it was Misty, but she still had yet to call him back. Could something be wrong?

"What's up?" he asked as he tossed his tools back into the cab of his truck.

"Rick has been released," she said, and he could hear the dogs at the shelter barking in the background. "His wife finally bailed him out."

"When was he released?" Brice asked, his mind immediately going to Misty. Could Rick have shown up at her house, and that's why she wasn't answering?

"Early this morning," Tori replied. Sounding a bit worried, she added, "He knows that Misty and I were at Daniel's café the night he was killed, and he also knows that we saw the killer."

His brow furrowing, Bruce said, "But you didn't actually see who it was."

"I know, but what if he thinks we did?" Tori sighed. "I think I'm going to go stay at Mom and Dad's tonight. I tried to call Misty, but she isn't answering. Are you at her house yet?"

"I'm heading there now," Brice said as he

jumped into his truck and cranked the engine.

"Tell her she's welcome to stay with us if she wants," Tori said. "It might be for the best; she's so isolated and alone all the way out there."

Brice nodded. "I'll tell her."

They hung up, and Brice pushed his truck to go faster, anxious to get to Misty's house as soon as possible. Knowing that Rick was on the loose put him on edge, and the quicker he could be at Misty's side, the better.

A shadowy figure walked slowly onto Misty's front porch and pulled the note from her front door, his hands steady as he read the scribbled words, *Gone to Mr. Thomas's – phone is dead.*

He wadded the paper into a ball and stuffed it in his pocket, a smile pulling at his lips as he turned and headed back toward his vehicle. This was perfect; he couldn't have planned it better if he'd tried. He cranked his car and headed toward old Mr. Thomas's cabin just as the sound of thunder rumbled in the distance.

Misty had just finished unloading the chest of drawers and was about to start in on the dresser when she glanced toward the closet and decided to get that task out of the way. She hadn't been able to fit many boxes into her car, and thought that she might have just enough for his clothes and shoes.

When she opened the closet door, she was surprised to find only a few shirts and pants, one jacket, and three pairs of shoes. The space, it seemed, was mostly occupied by several boxes stacked along the floor against the wall, along with a can of red spray paint.

"So, it *was* Mr. Thomas who left that message on my wall," she gasped under her breath as she leaned over to pick up the can. He'd apparently wanted her out of the house quite badly, but why?

Sinking to her knees, Misty pulled out a couple of the boxes and looked inside to find that they were filled with old bills, tax papers, and bank statements. She shoved them out to the middle of the room to be loaded into her car when she noticed that the last box was different. It was taped shut with "Do Not Open" scribbled in black marker on top. Unable to contain her curiosity, Misty pulled her keys from her pocket and cut the box open. What she found inside made her eyes widen.

The box was filled with old letters and photographs, and as Misty pulled them out to inspect them closer, she realized the letters were from Cora Griffin's grandmother. From what she could gather, Mr. Thomas courted her before she was married, and it was apparent by the words he'd written that he loved her deeply.

Dear Loren, Cora's grandmother wrote in her

last letter to Mr. Thomas, *I've spent the last week in utter agony as I've tried to decide what to do. I love you very much, you know that, but I also love Will and as much as it pains me to have to choose between the two of you, I must choose him. You've been so patient with me, and it kills me to hurt you this way, but I hope you can understand.*

Misty folded the letter and placed it back into the envelope, not wishing to intrude further on this romance that had once burned so brightly but was reduced to ashes. So, now she knew why he'd wanted her to leave the house; he'd wanted his memories to be left in peace. Poor Mr. Thomas. Misty wondered why he'd continued to work for the Griffins and realized how much he must have suffered while watching Cora's grandmother live her life with another man. Was that why he acted so bitter and later became such a recluse? Misty's heart squeezed in her chest; she wished she'd known. Maybe she could have befriended him and helped him somehow.

With a heavy sigh, she began placing everything back into the box when she noticed a group of more recent photographs stuffed against the side of the box. Pulling the pictures out, Misty looked through them and realized they'd been taken at some kind of party held at the bed-and-breakfast. Mr. Thomas was the primary focus of each picture, and she assumed it must have been his birthday.

Misty was about to return the pictures to the box when a few familiar faces caught her eye and she paused, eyeing the picture closer. The main focus was Mr. Thomas and his birthday cake, but Cora could be seen standing in the background surrounded by several of her friends, one of which was Hank. One particular person, however, was standing off to the side by himself. He apparently hadn't known he was in the picture, and the look of hate on his face as he glared at Cora made Misty's blood curdle. Flipping through the pictures more slowly this time, Misty found one more photo with him in it, and this time he and Cora were standing in the corner by themselves. Both of them looked angry, and he had his hand wrapped firmly around her upper arm, as if refusing to let her go.

Glancing into the lower corner of the picture, Misty realized this was only a few days before Cora was killed, and she felt the blood drain from her face. Standing slowly to her feet, she tried to figure out what all of this meant, but couldn't make any sense of it. If Cora and Hank were engaged, why would she have been arguing with *him?* In fact, why would he have even been invited to the party in the first place?

Suddenly, Misty heard the sound of an approaching vehicle, and she realized with a sigh of relief that it must be Brice. She'd been hearing the distant rumbles of thunder and knew that it would begin storming soon, and she wanted to get the boxes loaded into the car as quickly as possible.

The front door opened with a squeak, and the sound of footsteps bumped slowly along the hardwood floor.

"I'm in here, Brice," Misty called out from the bedroom.

The footsteps drew closer, and Misty was bent over stuffing Mr. Thomas's shirts into the last remaining box when a shadow fell over her. All at once, Misty saw the sneaker style boots and knew that her visitor was not Brice.

CHAPTER 20

Slowly raising her gaze upward, the hair stood up on the back of Misty's neck at the sinister smile and cold eyes that glinted back at her. This was the same man from the picture that now rested in her pocket, and she wondered how she hadn't seen the evil that lurked within his eyes before.

"Craig," she said in a choked whisper. "What are you doing here?"

Stepping closer, Craig reached out and pulled the photo from Misty's pocket and unfolded it. He gazed at it for a moment and then raised his eyes to stare back at Misty.

"You've figured it out, haven't you?" he asked, and when Misty didn't answer, he burst into laughter. "You're pretty smart, Miss Raven. I knew it the moment I saw you, which is why I've been trying so hard to get rid of you."

"Why did you do it?" Misty wanted to know as she slowly backed away from him. "Why did you kill Cora?"

A dark look passed over Craig's face, and Misty felt her blood run cold. "She deserved to die," he spat angrily. "Harlem Lewis wasn't her only secret boyfriend, you know. Before I went off to college, she was dating *me.* She said she loved me and would wait for me, but she lied."

"W-weren't you a bit young for her?" Misty asked hesitantly, her brow furrowing.

Glaring at her, Craig said, "I was almost eighteen, and she was twenty-three, which is the reason we kept it quiet. We agreed we would make our relationship public when I got my two-year associate degree and came home, but while I was away, do you know what she did? She dumped me for my brother!"

He started laughing then, uncontrollably, and Misty eyed the door, mentally trying to gauge whether she could get out of the house. Craig blocked her way, and she knew she couldn't get past him; she had to keep him talking until she could figure out something else.

"Did your brother know about your relationship with Cora?" she asked.

Craig stopped laughing then and nodded, a malicious smile curving his lips upward. "Yes, he did, which is why it felt so good when I heard Cora dumped him, the same way she did me. She didn't care about any of us; all she cared about was herself."

"It seemed like she cared for Hank," Misty stated, trying to keep her expression neutral when her eyes landed on a golf club in Mr. Thomas's closet. "Wasn't she going to marry him?"

His jaw clenching, Craig said stiffly, "She said she was, but then they broke up. I tried to get her back, you know, and she rejected me. She said that she truly loved Hank, and asked me to leave her alone."

"But you didn't?" Misty asked as she slowly edged her way closer to the closet, hoping that Craig wouldn't notice.

With a humorless laugh, Craig shook his head. "Of course I didn't," he stated. "If I couldn't have her, I had no intention of letting anyone else take her."

"So, you killed her and made it look like a suicide," Misty said matter-of-factly. "Did you know Hank was coming over that night to see her?"

"No, that was a surprise," he said with a sigh. Shrugging casually, he added, "But I was glad to get rid of him, too."

This man was a maniac. How had Misty not realized that before? It seemed, though, that she wasn't the only person to be deceived; he'd been deceiving the whole town for fifteen years.

Misty had almost made it to the closet door when Craig looked at her and said with an evil grin, "Now it's time to get rid of *you*, Misty Raven. You've been a thorn in my flesh since your arrival, and now I'm going to put an end to you."

"You won't get away with it," Misty said, her heart kicking into overdrive. "With Rick in jail, everyone will be looking at *you*, Craig."

Chuckling, Craig shook his head and began to walk slowly around the room. "They've released my brother on bail, Misty," he said. "So, don't you see? It's the perfect set-up. He gets out of jail, you tune up dead, the police will find enough evidence to convict him, and he'll be put away for good."

"He's your brother, Craig," Misty said in disbelief. "How could you do that to him?"

Spinning around to face her, Craig's face was a mask of anger as he spat, "Why should I care about him when all he's ever done for me is stomp my face into the ground? He's hated me ever since I was born, and I'll be glad to see him finally get what's coming to him."

Without warning, Craig lunged across the room at Misty, his hands reaching for her throat and his eyes ablaze with hate and fury. Her heart pounding, Misty dove toward the golf club and gripped the cold metal in her hand, spinning to swing it at Craig's head with all her might. The club whistled through the air above his head with a *whoosh* as Craig ducked, and before Misty could swing again, he was upon her.

"Did you think I didn't see the golf club?" he hissed as he wrapped his fingers tightly around her throat. "Cora, Hank, nor Daniel outsmarted me, so how did you think you could?"

What Craig didn't realize was that Misty still clutched the golf club, and with one quick jab, she thrust it into his side. With a moan, Craig loosened his grip around her throat just enough for Misty to get free. Shoving him back as hard as she could, Misty ran toward the door, her only thought that of escape. If she could only get to her car, she could get away from him and find help.

She'd just made it to the doorway when she heard him regain his footing and come after her, the pounding of his footsteps louder than the pounding of her heart. He reached her just as she passed over the threshold and grabbed her by the hair, yanking her backward. She continued to fight, and out of the corner of her eye, Misty saw his hand resting against the doorframe, and she quickly grabbed the door and slammed it on his exposed fingers. With a howl, he released her hair and she lunged toward her car.

Suddenly, with a feeling of despair, Misty realized she'd left her keys lying on the closet floor next to the boxes, and her heart sank as her only hope of escape disappeared along the breeze. Knowing she didn't have long to think, Misty did the first thing that came to her mind; she ran toward the small, wooded pathway that led to her house. Perhaps if she could get home, Wally would be able to protect her.

The day had grown darker with the approaching storm, and Misty could barely see as she hurried along the overgrown path. She could hear him coming behind her, and she pushed herself to go faster, ignoring the tree branches and bushes that grabbed at her hair and clothes like grasping, ghostly fingers.

"You can run, but you can't hide," Craig called out from behind, his laughter echoing through the forest.

Her lungs felt as if they would explode, and Misty wondered if she'd be able to make it. Craig was a man and most likely faster, but she wouldn't give up. She couldn't give up; she knew what awaited her if she did.

He no longer called out, and when branches and twigs began to snap to her right, she jerked her head in that direction, searching the dark, dense forest. Had Craig left the path and was circling around to meet her head on? Fear forced her to press on, but she knew in her heart that she wouldn't be able to make it.

Thunder rumbled overhead, shaking the ground beneath Misty's feet. The air was icy cold, but sweat dripped from her forehead as she continued to run. All of the sudden, she caught a glimpse of light just up ahead, and she realized with a jolt of hope that she was almost at the end of the path. Just a few more feet and she'd be in her backyard.

"I've got you now!"

Craig leaped from the forest like a large, black falcon, his claws reaching out once again to wrap around her throat. Misty screamed and tried to fight him, but she was much weaker this time, and as his fingers squeezed tighter and tighter, she felt the life begin to fade from her body.

Suddenly, another shadow loomed from behind and struck Craig on the back of the neck. Misty fell to the ground as Craig let her go, the forest floor swirling wildly before her eyes. She could hear scuffling and panting and the rustling of feet against leaves and twigs, but she couldn't seem to focus. Her heart raced, her lungs ached, and her limbs felt lifeless.

With a loud *thud,* a body hit the ground and all was silent. Misty couldn't see who slowly moved to stand over her, and she was almost afraid to look. Was Craig coming back to finish the job?

"Misty, are you alright?"

Tears of relief filled her eyes at the sound of Brice's voice, and she pushed herself to her knees just as he kneeled beside her.

"C-Craig?" she asked, gripping Brice's hand like a lifeline.

"He's dead, Misty."

CHAPTER 21

Misty stared at Brice in shock, her mind desperately trying to process everything that had happened. Her body felt limp and drained, as if she'd just climbed the highest mountain or swam the largest ocean, and she found it hard to focus. With tears in her eyes, Misty clutched Brice's hand and struggled to stand, but found her legs to be too weak.

"He pulled a knife on me, and when I hit him, he fell on it," Brice explained as he pulled Misty up, and she forced herself not to look at the body that lay limp and lifeless only a few feet away. "What on earth happened? It looked like he was trying to strangle you when I came up."

"I'll tell you everything," she said, her voice weak. "Just please, help me get home."

Brice all but carried Misty through the remainder of the woods and into her house. As he helped her sit down at the kitchen table, Wally immediately ran to her side and began sniffing at her hands and arms, as if trying to figure out what was wrong. With trembling fingers, Misty gently stroked his head while Brice called the police.

"They'll be here in a few minutes," he said after ending the call. Coming to sit by Misty, he looked at her with concern and asked, "Are you alright? Can I get you anything?"

"I'm fine," she replied, her smile a bit too wobbly to be of much reassurance. "How…how on earth did you find me?"

"I had a flat tire, which is why I was late in the first place, and I had just gotten to your house when I heard you scream." Brice stopped and ran his fingers through his hair, shaking his head as he sighed heavily. "I think my blood started running in the wrong direction; you sounded absolutely terrified. I figured it was Rick that was after you since Tori called to tell me he'd been released on bail, so was I ever surprised to find Craig with his hands around your throat."

"He killed them, Brice," Misty said softly. "Cora, Hank, Daniel…all of them."

The sound of approaching sirens interrupted their conversation, and Brice hurried through the house to let the police inside. The next hour was excruciating; Officer Lewis asked question after question while his men retrieved the body from the woods, and Misty could see the doubt and suspicion in his eyes as she explained what had happened.

"I'm sorry, Miss Raven, but unless you have more proof, I'm going to have to take you in," he finally said once she'd finished.

"Harlem, the man was trying to strangle her," Brice spoke up in disbelief. "What more proof do you need?"

Turning his piercing stare on Brice, Officer Lewis stated, "You're going to have to come, too, Brice. You killed a man today, and I'm afraid we're going to have to hold you until we can get more evidence."

"Officer Lewis, why don't you believe us?" Misty cried in frustration.

"Because no one in this town ever heard anything about Cora and Craig having a secret relationship," he snapped, "and frankly, I think you made it up."

"No, she didn't," a voice spoke out, and they all turned in surprise to find Rick Harley standing in the doorway. "It's true; they *did* date."

His eyebrows raised, Harlem asked, "I suppose you can prove that?"

"Yes, I can," Rick nodded, his face solemn. "Craig has a whole picture album of the two of them in his bedroom, along with a bloodstained sweater that Cora was apparently wearing the night she died. I found it all a couple of years after Cora's death, and Craig confessed the whole thing."

"Why didn't you tell the police then?" Officer Lewis asked, his voice full of doubt.

Sighing, Rick replied, "I could say because we were brothers, but that's not exactly true. Daniel Abraham was blackmailing me, and I blackmailed Craig in return."

Glancing at Misty and Brice, Officer Lewis asked, "Are you sure you want to discuss this now,

Rick, without your attorney?"

"Yes," Rick nodded his head. "It's time everyone knew the truth."

Rick came to sit at the table with Misty and Brice, and Officer Lewis joined them, a notepad and pencil in his hand.

"Do you remember the hit-and-run accident that killed Korey Newton?" Rick asked, looking over at Harlem. When he received a nod of confirmation, he continued, "I was the driver that hit him. I'd been drinking that night, and I knew I'd go to prison if I stuck around, so I ran. Daniel Abraham saw the whole thing." He stopped and lowered his head, but not before Misty saw the guilt in his eyes. "He came to me later and threatened to turn me in if I didn't give him money, so I told him all I could afford was fifteen thousand dollars. He almost turned me down, but then I guess he figured he wouldn't get anything if I went to prison, so he agreed. I didn't know, however, that he would expect fifteen thousand dollars every year."

Rick stood up then and walked slowly around the kitchen, his hands pushed deep into his pockets as he spoke. "When I found out about Craig's secret, I used it to my advantage. Any time I needed help with my plumbing business, I had a free worker, and whenever I needed repairs done around the house, he would see to it. It really wasn't such a bad deal for him, considering the alternative, but my pushing him around drove him crazy. I knew when Miss Raven came into town and the body was discovered, it would only be a matter of time." Turning to look at Misty, he said, "I'm sorry I got so angry with you before, Miss Raven, and I'm sorry for what my brother did to you. Neither of us is any good; I guess we never were."

"What about Daniel Abraham?" Misty wanted to know. "Did Craig kill him, too?"

Rick nodded. "Yes, he did," he replied. "He found out about the blackmail and thought that if he got rid of Daniel, he could take his place and turn the tables on me."

"How can we know that's true?" Brice asked skeptically.

"When we did Daniel's autopsy, we found skin under his fingernails from where he apparently scratched the murderer while trying to get away," Officer Lewis stated. "Rick here had a few scratches on his neck, which is one reason we arrested him, but the DNA didn't match. We'll check Craig's body for any scratches and see if his DNA matches."

After everything had been said, Rick leaned against the sink and sighed, as if utterly exhausted and depleted of life, and Officer Lewis took his arm and led him outside to his patrol car. Misty watched them go, hardly able to believe everything that had happened since her arrival to Shady Pines, and now knowing that it was all finally over, she felt exhausted, as well.

"So, Cora can rest in peace now that everyone

finally knows the truth," Brice said, reaching up to rub the back of his neck. Shaking his head, he added incredulously, "I can't believe all of this has been going on for the last fifteen years. First, Cora is murdered and everyone thinks it was suicide, Hank disappears, Rick kills someone in a hit and run, Daniel starts blackmailing Rick, and then Rick blackmails his own brother. What a crazy town I grew up in!"

"It's hard to believe, isn't it?" Misty shook her head and sighed. With a grateful smile, she reached out and squeezed his arm. "Thank you, Brice, for saving my life. If there's anything I can ever do for you, please let me know."

Gazing warmly back at Misty, Brice took her hand and said, "There actually *is* something you can do."

"What's that?" Misty asked, tilting her head to the side.

With a glint in his eye, he replied, "You can stay in Shady Pines."

Misty pulled her hand away and stood up to fix herself a cup of coffee. "Oh, I don't know, Brice," she said uncertainly. "I've never stayed in one place for very long, and there are things…well, that I still have to figure out."

Brice stood up and came to stand beside Misty. "Do these "things" have anything to do with your childhood?" he asked, his tone serious. "Or that locket you keep around your neck?"

Glancing at him in surprise, Misty hesitated

before answering, not quite sure what to say. She'd never confided in anyone before, but she knew now that she could trust Brice. He had, after all, just saved her life, hadn't he?

With a sigh, Misty finally nodded. "Yes." She went to sit back at the table with a hot cup of coffee in her hand and, taking the locket off, handed it to Brice and said, "For as long as I can remember, I had a little Winnie the Pooh teddy bear I carried with me everywhere I went; I had it with me when the preacher man handed me over to the authorities in Atlanta, and I guess I found it to be a source of comfort somehow." Misty's mind was filled with memories as she watched Brice open the locket and peer inside. "About eight years ago, I decided to have it cleaned and re-stuffed, and the lady that did it for me called to tell me there was something sewn inside."

Looking at Misty in surprise, Brice asked, "You mean, this locket was inside of your bear?"

"Yes," Misty nodded, "and I never knew it."

Brice studied the black-and-white photo of a young woman looking down at the baby she held, and after a moment he asked, "Do you think this is your mother?"

Misty shrugged. "I think so, but I can't know for sure. I wish I could see her face better; her hair blocks most of her features."

She reached out and took the locket from him to pull the tiny picture gently from its encasement. Turning it around, she pointed to the small, scribbled message written on the back and said, "It says here on the back: *Look for me in the sky.* See?"

Brice looked at the message, his brow furrowing as he asked, "What do you think it means? Do you suppose she was sick and knew she was about to die, and that's why she left you at the church?"

"I just don't know," Misty sighed. Her gaze intense, she looked at Brice and said, "What if it's more than that? What if she was in danger and couldn't explain why she left me, so she wrote a message with a hidden meaning that I'm supposed to figure out?"

"Like what?" Brice asked, studying Misty with his dark blue eyes.

"Well, "the sky" could be symbolic of something, like a big city with skyscrapers, or a particular street with the word sky in it."

"You could be right," he said, nodding his head thoughtfully. A light suddenly dawning in his eyes, Brice sat up straighter, studying Misty closely as he said, "One of the streets here in town is called Skyland Drive. Is that why you came to Shady Pines, Misty?"

Smiling sheepishly, Misty nodded and said, "Yes, and because I stumbled upon a newspaper clipping about the disappearances of those girls twenty-five years ago."

Brice looked confused. "But you acted like you didn't know anything about that?"

"Yes, well, I've learned not to act like I know too

much or people get suspicious and won't tell me anything at all," Misty replied. "But I didn't know about the disappearance of their Spanish teacher until I got here."

"You mean you've done this sort of thing before?"

Misty nodded. "Eight times before. The minute I discovered that locket, I sold my house and began my search. I haven't found anything so far, but maybe I will someday."

Reaching out to take her hand, Brice squeezed it gently and said, "I know you will, Misty."

They were sitting close to each other at the table, and when Brice didn't move his hand, Misty looked up at him and their eyes met. In the depths of his beautiful blue gaze, Misty saw something there that made her heart catch, and it seemed to her that he leaned a bit closer.

Before she could decide whether or not to move away, Misty heard the front door open and Tori called out, "Misty, are you here? I heard what happened and came right over!"

Brice immediately moved back, and with a chuckle, Misty shook her head and said, "You sure can't keep a secret for long in a small town."

CHAPTER 22

A week passed, and everything was finally starting to feel more normal again. The town was still chattering about Craig and Rick and everything in between; it wasn't often that such a crime was committed in a small town like Shady Pines, and Misty knew they'd be talking about it for years to come.

It was Saturday morning, and Misty rose early to get ready for an outing with Brice. After Craig's death, she'd made the statement that now her porch swing would never get done, and Brice said he knew of an elderly gentleman in a neighboring town that made custom swings as a hobby.

"What's the name of this town again?" Misty asked when he arrived at her house.

Opening the truck door for her, he said, "Cloud Haven. I'm sure you've never heard of it; it's a tiny little town with only about five hundred or so people who live there."

Circling around to the driver's side, Brice climbed into the truck and they started toward Cloud Haven. As they drove, Misty attempted to make small talk, but Brice was very quiet and didn't seem to be in the mood for talking. She finally gave up and gazed out the window at the passing scenery, her mind wandering to everything that needed to be done at the house before the renovations would be through.

After they'd been driving for a while, Brice cleared his throat and said, "I didn't get a chance to say this last Saturday, but thank you for telling me about the locket and your search to find the truth about your past. I…well, since you entrusted me with something so important, I'd like to tell you a little about my past, as well."

Misty glanced at him in surprise, her eyebrows raising in question as she asked, "Oh?"

"Yes," he nodded, keeping his eyes trained on the road ahead. "Five years ago, I was engaged to a girl named Cassie. We grew up together and I'd been crazy for her since high school, so when she finally agreed to date me, I was over the moon. Three weeks before the wedding, I went over to her house to pick her up for a date when I noticed a note stuck on the front door."

Brice paused, his jaw clenching, and Misty could hear the pain in his voice. She waited patiently for him to continue, all the while wondering what had happened.

Finally, with a sigh, he said, "She ran off with Matt, my best friend *and* best man, and I haven't seen either of them since."

"I'm so sorry, Brice," Misty said softly, her heart going out to him. "That had to be very hard."

"Other than my dad's death, it was the hardest thing I've ever gone through," he replied. "I haven't dated anyone since then, and…well, I'm not sure I ever will."

Misty knew what he was trying to say, and with a smile, she said, "I understand. I would tell you to move on with your life and find happiness, but who am I to give advice? I can't move on with my life either until I know more about my past."

"What a pair we make," he replied with a wry grin. "While you're trying to find your past, I'm running away from mine."

Misty laughed. "Well, maybe someday we'll both get everything straightened out and be able to move on with our lives." With a mischievous glint in her eyes, she looked over at Brice and added, "For a minute there, I thought you were going to say that you also dated Cora Griffin."

Laughing, Brice shook his head and said, "Considering I was only fifteen when she died, that would be a negative."

The mood between them lightened after that, and by the time they made it to Cloud Haven, they were back to their usual joking, teasing ways. As Brice slowed down to enter the tiny town, Misty gazed out of her window at the old, charming buildings they passed. Something about this place seemed vaguely familiar, but Misty shook it off and just assumed it was because it resembled so many other small towns in America.

Brice pulled up in front of a small store at the end of the block and parked, and the two went inside. The smell of wood wafted beneath Misty's nose as soon as they entered, and she gazed around at the beautiful, handcrafted pieces of work displayed around the small area.

"Does he do much business in a town this size?" Misty whispered.

"He ships a lot of it out," Brice replied, pointing to a gorgeous rocking chair made from oak. "He does it mainly as just a hobby now that he's retired."

An elderly gentleman stepped from the back room then, wearing an old plaid shirt, a baseball cap, and a sweater. He was small-framed and his shoulders were stooped with age, but his eyes were sharp and twinkled with good humor.

"Brice, my boy, it's good to see you," he greeted Brice in a raspy voice. Looking at Misty, he smiled pleasantly and said, "Welcome to my shop, young lady. I'm Joe Caddel."

"It's so nice to meet you, Mr. Caddel," Misty said, introducing herself. "Brice has told me what beautiful work you do, and I see he was right."

Waving his hand in the air, Mr. Caddel said, "Oh, Brice exaggerates, but thank you. And please, call me Joe."

The three discussed Misty's order for a porch swing, and by the time they were through, she'd also ordered two rocking chairs, a linen closet for one of the bathrooms, a coffee table, and a rustic coat rack for the front hall.

"Are you certain I don't owe you more?" Misty asked in surprise when Joe told her the price.

"Positive," he replied with a grin. "I don't have

anything better to do with my time, and besides, you're a friend of Brice's, so I gave you a discount."

"That is so kind of you," she said, her heart warming as she handed him her credit card. "Thank you, Joe."

Just then, the bell above the door jingled, and a tall young man around Misty's age walked in carrying a to-go box.

"Here's your lunch, Grandad," he said, and Misty noticed his eyes were the same shade of hazel as Joe's. Smiling at Brice, he nodded and said, "Hey, Barlow. How's it going?"

"Chris, I'd like you to meet this charming young lady that probably just spent her life's savings on some custom-made items," Joe said, chuckling as he waved his grandson over. "Chris, this is Misty Raven. She's living over in Shady Pines now."

"It's very nice to meet you, Misty," Chris said, coming over to shake her hand. He had a head full of thick, reddish-brown hair and a very attractive smile.

"It's nice to meet you, too," she replied. Her eyes sparkling, she added, "And I didn't spend my life's savings because your grandfather didn't charge me nearly enough."

"He's always had a soft spot for a pretty face," he said with a grin.

"Is that barbecue from the Rusty Pig?" Brice interrupted, motioning toward the box Chris held. The aroma of fresh, hot barbecue drifted from around the edges, and Misty felt her stomach rumble.

"It is," Chris nodded. "They've got homemade red velvet cake for dessert today, too."

Wiggling his eyebrows at Misty, Brice asked, "Ready for lunch?"

Misty nodded eagerly, and after saying their goodbyes, the two headed across the street to the Rusty Pig. The restaurant was small, with only enough room for three tables, but an elderly couple was vacating one when they entered, and Brice quickly grabbed it.

The meal was delicious, and the red velvet cake was every bit as wonderful as Misty expected. For such a small town, she was surprised at the number of people who came in for to-go orders, but the food was so exceptional she assumed that people from neighboring towns also stopped by.

Brice insisted he pay for everything, and as they walked out, Misty thanked him.

"And not only for the delicious meal," she said, "but also for driving me over here. I never would have found it on my own, and I'm so excited about the items I ordered!"

Brice chuckled as he opened his truck door for her. "You're quite welcome."

As they drove back through town, Brice turned down a side street and Misty asked him where he was going.

"This is just a different way out of town," he replied, and she looked out the window, surprised to find several more shops dotting the sidewalks.

Just down the block, Misty spotted the steeple of a church peaking up over the rooftops, and she felt her heart jump a little. Her brow furrowing, she stared at it as they drew nearer, trying to figure out what was making her react so.

The church came into view, its rustic outer walls painted stark white, and Misty felt a strange sense of Déjà vu. Suddenly, a scene flashed before her eyes, and she caught her breath, squeezing her eyes shut. Just like in her dreams, she saw lights flashing overhead and could hear the sound of heavy breathing and feet pounding against the pavement. Something always rose up through the darkness, but Misty had never been able to make out what it was.

Until now.

This time, she saw it; a church steeple, standing stark white against a dark sky as a black-haired woman ran toward it with Misty in her arms. She'd never been able to see the person's face in her dreams, but now the blurry profile of a beautiful young woman drifted before Misty's eyes, and through the haze, she sensed that the woman was very afraid.

Opening her eyes, Misty realized they'd already passed the church, and she grabbed Brice's arm and cried, "Brice, stop!"

Brice slammed on the brakes and looked at her in surprise. "What's wrong?"

Not saying a word, Misty climbed from the truck

and slowly walked to stand before the church, her mind whirling. She'd seen this church before, long ago on a cold, dark night. She could hear voices speaking in muted conversation, but couldn't quite grasp the words, and she clutched her head as if trying to squeeze the memories out.

"Misty, what's wrong?" Brice asked as he hurried to her side. "Are you alright?"

Turning to look at him, almost in a daze, she said slowly, "Brice, I've been here before."

His brow wrinkling in confusion, he asked, "To this church?"

"Yes," she nodded, the moment feeling very surreal. Reaching out to clutch his arm, she said, "This is *the* church, Brice. Don't you see? This is where my mother left me, and this is what she meant in her message, *Look for me in the sky.* The name of this town is Cloud Haven!"

His eyes widening in shock, it took Brice a moment to respond. "Are...are you sure?" he asked in a near whisper.

Nodding once again, Misty turned to look back at the old, familiar structure and said, "Yes, I'm sure. It's starting to come back, Brice. I can see a woman, whom I assume to be my mother, carrying me here."

"Can you remember anything else?" he asked.

With a sigh, Misty shook her head. "No, not yet." Turning to face him, she said in a low, serious tone, "But I know this much, Brice. If my mother really was that Spanish teacher, I don't think she just disappeared; I think she was murdered, and I've got to find out why."

A NOTE FROM THE AUTHOR

Thank you so much for reading the first book of "A Shady Pines Mystery" series. If you enjoyed it, please leave a review on Amazon or Goodreads – or both! I look forward to hearing from you, and I can't wait for you to read book #2 - *Lost in the Past*

To visit my website and sign up for my newsletter, please visit
www.jennyelaineauthor.com

Lost in the Past
A Shady Pines Mystery, Book 2

Mysterious dreams, a haunting past, and a dangerous secret. Is it too late for the truth to be uncovered?

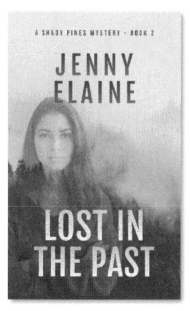

Twenty-five years ago, four women mysteriously disappeared from the small town of Shady Pines, Georgia. The police investigated, but there was never any suspicion of foul play. Now, Misty Raven is trying to find the truth of what happened, but someone is desperate to stop her. When Misty's life is threatened and a beloved citizen is found dead, she knows it's just a matter of time before she's next. Dive into this delightful, spine-tingling sequel as Misty fights to uncover the secrets from the past.

Storms of the Past
A Shady Pines Mystery, Book 3

"Legend has it that when the black wolf is spotted, death is sure to follow."

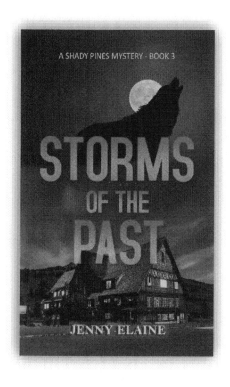

Years ago, in the hills of North Georgia, the Indians told a story of a lone black wolf that emerged from the smoke of revenge. The story became a legend, and now when the wolf is seen, it is said that someone will die.

After learning her mother once lived in Dahlonega, Misty travels to Black Wolf Lodge in search of answers. While there, a deadly storm sweeps through the mountains, ravaging the area and trapping everyone at the lodge. When one of the guests is killed, the legend of the black wolf is blamed, but Misty feels there could be a murderer lurking in their midst. As she delves into the secrets of the lodge, buried truths come to light and mysteries of the past are finally revealed.

THE HEALING ROSE
OF SAVANNAH

ROSE OF SAVANNAH SERIES – BOOK 1

While seeking solace from a broken heart, Savannah Rose travels to the picturesque city of Savannah, Georgia, only to find herself trapped within the confines of romance, murder, and mystery. It is the 1940's, a war is being waged in Europe, and a serial killer stalks the streets of Savannah, targeting young women and terrorizing the city. When the killer sets his sights on Savannah Rose, she must fight to survive, and in an attempt to save her life, she journeys away from the city only to encounter tragedy and more heartbreak. Forced to return home and face the danger that continues to lurk among the shadows, Savannah Rose struggles to overcome the obstacles thrown into her path. Along the way, she searches for healing, discovers the real meaning of life, and finds her one true love. Blended with rich history and creative storytelling, this suspenseful saga sweeps readers back and forth between the 1940's and the 1960's,and will keep you captivated until its final conclusion.

"What a wonderful book. It kept my attention the whole time and I had no clue of how it would end, until the last page!! Thoroughly enjoyed it!"
-Goodreads review

"This is an amazing story full of mystery, romance, and suspense. It was such a great read, I could hardly put it down!"
-Goodreads review

"A very good and moving story line. Enjoyed the book and the history. Some laughs and tears. Good read for a raining day."
-Amazon review

"Loved this book! Enjoyed the shift between '40's & 60s'. This story had it all: mystery, romance, humor, sorrow, a prominent family's secret and twists I never saw coming. I hated to see it end and wish a sequel was in the works."
-Amazon review

THE WHISPERING SHADOWS OF SAVANNAH

ROSE OF SAVANNAH SERIES – BOOK 2

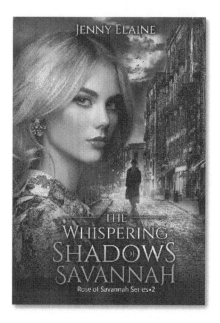

It is the 1940s, and Vivian McCombs witnesses a horrible crime on the outskirts of Savannah, Georgia. When no one will believe her story, she is accused of being responsible for the crime and sent away. Desperate to prove her innocence, Vivian is forced to endure the chaos that has overtaken her life. Upon her return home three months later, Vivian befriends Eva Beckett, a young immigrant who is struggling to support her family after the death of her husband. When strange things begin to occur, both women must fight to conquer the dangers that lurk among the whispering shadows.

Follow the lives of these two brave women as they form friendships, search for healing, gather strength to overcome life's obstacles, and find love along the way. The alluring history of Savannah will captivate you in this astounding story of mystery, courage, romance, and suspense.

"A wonderful 2nd book in this series. It was attention-grabbing from the beginning! I found it hard to put down and read it from cover to cover within about 6 hours."
-Amazon Review

"Once again, I was blown away by the author and her ability to write such captivating, real-life moments and do it in a way that left me breathless. It was incredibly well-written and impossible not to picture the scenes playing out as I read along."
-Amazon Review

"Great read!! I thoroughly enjoyed this book. If you like romance, mystery, and historical fiction you will love this book."
-Goodreads Review

Made in the USA
Middletown, DE
17 July 2023